The Streets Have No Queen

The Streets Have No Queen

JaQuavis Coleman

www.urbanbooks.net

Urban Books, LLC
300 Farmingdale Road, N.Y.-Route 109
Farmingdale, NY 11735

The Streets Have No Queen

ISBN 13: 978-1-64556-154-5
ISBN 10: 1-64556-154-2

First Trade Paperback Printing March 2021
Printed in the United States of America

10 9 8 7 6 5 4 3 2 1

This is a work of fiction. Any references or similarities to actual events, real people, living or dead, or to real locales are intended to give the novel a sense of reality. Any similarity in other names, characters, places, and incidents is entirely coincidental.

Distributed by Kensington Publishing Corp.
Submit Orders to:
Customer Service
400 Hahn Road
Westminster, MD 21157-4627
Phone: 1-800-733-3000
Fax: 1-800-659-2436

The Streets Have No Queen

by

JaQuavis Coleman

This isn't a sequel, but a well thought-out puzzle.
Everything connects. It always does.

—JaQuavis Coleman

Prologue

A man lay comfortably on a brown leather couch, intensely staring at the ceiling. He had little to no movement as his eyes were fixated on a small imperfection on the surface. His head was slightly propped up by a small pillow. The room was quiet. Well, almost. Nothing but the constant sound of the steel balls clinking as they swung back and forth on the pendulum filled the air. Most people called this Newton's cradle. It caused a constant ticking echo throughout the dim room. A brown hue from the desk lamp hovered over the office, and the faint smell of vanilla danced around. Hundreds of books lined the bookshelves against the walls. A woman sat off in a corner with a notepad in hand, studying the man on the couch. She watched his every move.

"At first . . ." the man said in a low tone just before pausing. He took a deep breath, cleared his throat, and clenched his jaw firmly. He was trying his hardest to fight off tears, and he took a hard swallow. He inhaled deeply and slowly exhaled, almost as if he could release some of the pain he had built up in his chest by merely blowing it out. He closed his eyes and began to speak again. "At first, she asked if we could jump with no plan. I said, 'Fuck it. I'm with it.' I was all in," the man said, choosing his words wisely as they came out.

"They say love is exactly like skydiving. If you really think about it, that's some real shit. Love is a fucking free fall. You truly don't have any control over the final outcome once you've committed to love someone. Shit's crazy, right? Just think about it. You don't 'walk in love' and you don't 'run in love.' You fucking *fall* in love. That's what her love was like. It always felt like I was falling. No control. No foundation. I was just falling. It was the greatest feeling in the world to me." As he lay back, a single tear slipped down his face, traveling down to the rim of his ear. The man quickly sat up and shook his head in grief.

"Bless, please continue," the doctor said as she gently tapped her pen on her notebook. The beautiful Dr. Celeste Ose was a Haitian-born psychiatrist. She had perfect ebony skin and high cheekbones. Her naturally kinky hair was pulled neatly into a bun on top of her head. She was slightly intrigued by Bless. He was so mysterious, and he was a man she couldn't quite understand. She repeated herself, eagerly wanting him to resume. "Please continue," Dr. Ose said.

Still, he said nothing. She had been seeing him for months, and he had never talked about her for more than a few sentences. She was seeing progress, and she wanted him to keep going to enable her to dig deeper. Dr. Ose paused and waited for a response. He remained quiet, and he seemed as if he was in deep thought, searching for the right thing to say.

"I can't. I just see red when I think about her. All I can see is red," Bless said as he shook his head in grief.

"I know it is upsetting and hurtful to lose a spouse, but the first step to healing is to—" the doctor said, but before she could finish her sentence, the man stood up and grabbed his blazer.

"I'm sorry, Doc. I have to go," he said as he gave her a forced grin. "I appreciate your time."

"I understand. I'll see you next week for our next session, correct?" Dr. Ose asked as she smiled back with understanding eyes.

"Yeah, sure. I will be back," Bless said in a low tone just before exiting the office, leaving her sitting there puzzled.

In all her years, she had never had a patient so complex and so hard to get a breakthrough from. Dr. Ose reached over to her desktop and stopped the Newton's cradle. She contemplated referring him to a different doctor to see if someone else could help him, but she chose to keep trying.

Bless had been coming to the doctor for six months straight, and their sessions never went more than ten minutes because of his unwillingness to talk about his deceased wife. He would start and just abruptly leave. Every . . . single . . . time. However, on that day, he spoke longer than he ever had before, and because of that, she knew he was making progress. Dr. Ose's professional integrity wanted to refer him elsewhere, but her greed stopped her. You see, Bless was a high-profile client. He paid in cash every week and always paid triple the invoice. His only requests were that his files be kept secret and he came after hours. It was obvious that he was a very private patient. She didn't know exactly what Bless did for a living, but by the way he paid, she knew he did it very well.

Bless got into the back seat of his luxury Maybach and instructed his driver to go to the cemetery. He wanted to talk to Queen, his deceased wife. He needed a release. He needed to talk to his best friend to try to find some sort of clarity. On that day, her death weighed heavily on his spirit, and he felt himself breaking down. Bless knew that death was a part of life, but the way she'd left him was something that he couldn't accept.

He watched aimlessly out his window as they maneuvered through the Detroit traffic. Although cars, nature, and pedestrians were in his eyeshot, the only thing he could see was the face of the love of his life. Her smile was what he would miss the most. The way her dimples were deep always made him smile. Queen had dimples so deep you could place nickels in them securely. Her chubby cheeks and her sweet smell would be things he would never forget.

Scattered pictures of Queen flashed in his mind, causing him to smile from ear to ear and randomly chuckle when he thought about the way she laughed. Her laugh could make any room a happy one. The twenty-minute ride seemed like only a minute or two because of his extended daydream. As the vehicle entered the cemetery, the pain began to slowly creep back into Bless's chest. He grabbed a small briefcase from the next seat and exited the car.

The closer he got to her grave, the more Bless could feel his wife's presence. It was a bittersweet feeling, because he could always feel his heart get heavier with each step when he made his way to his baby. The harsh reality that she was buried six feet underground plagued his thoughts. Bless finally approached where she rested, and he took a deep breath.

He looked at the three-foot tombstone and examined the wording. It read, MY EARTH. MY ISIS. MY QUEEN. FALL 1990–RISE 2018. The cemetery staff and tomb makers pleaded with Bless when they got the tombstone wording request. They tried to convince him that he had it backward. Every time, Bless would laugh and simply answer, "If you knew her, you would know it's one hundred percent correct." His wife and he would always talk about how loving each other was like falling, and he laughed at their inside joke, which the world didn't seem to get.

The cemetery's lawn was full of leaves, being that it was the middle of autumn. The trees were almost bare, and the light wind made small, beautiful tornados on various parts of the walkway. Bless approached the grave and rubbed his hand over her name. "My Queen. My Queen," he whispered as his eyes began to tear up. He had married his dream girl and found the love of his life. Not too many people live without regrets, but up until her death, Bless had none. He was happy, content, and free when he was with her. Queen understood him and he got her. They had been childhood classmates, and as they grew, so did their love. By high school, they had already vowed to each other that they would spend the rest of their lives together. The words "soul mate" didn't do their union any justice. Their bond was spiritual. Their bond was unbreakable.

Their bond was no more.

Bless pulled off his jacket and laid it over the grass. He sat down and began to open his briefcase. "Hey, pretty girl. I had a rough day today. Wanna hear about it?" he whispered as he wiped a tear away. He dug into the bag and pulled out a small blank canvas and a few paint brushes. He began to do his routine as he prepared to do a small painting while talking to her. This was something they'd done while she was alive. It had brought him peace then, and it seemed to do the same thing now.

Bless began to paint a picture while casually talking to his wife as if she were literally sitting there with him. An hour passed. He laughed, cried, and reminisced all while recreating the cemetery's scenery. The speckled orange and red leaves were scattered throughout the canvas with so much detail you could see the vines within the plants. Bless even added a small fox in the background to complement the aesthetics of his creation. He smiled knowing that Queen loved the way he always strategically did things and painted with precision. She would tell him he was like a mad scientist with his paintbrush. She had always been his number one fan.

Bless continued to paint until the sun began to set, and then he headed back to the car to get home. It had been a rough day for him. His days were up and down, and this particular day was a down one. He just wanted to go home and sleep the pain away. Sometimes you have to sleep and give your pain to God, and that was what his plans were for that evening.

The driver returned Bless to his home, and he immediately poured himself a glass of cognac and put on some jazz. The smooth and soothing sounds played throughout the house, and Bless began to unwind. He loosened his shirt and kicked off his shoes as he went to the back window that overlooked a pond. The moonlight bounced off the pond, and he stood there admiring the scene. Bless took a small sip of the aged cognac and closed his eyes as he savored the taste and the good music. He heard a sound of thunder, and shortly after, it began to rain. He smiled, remembering how Queen liked to make love when it rained. For some reason, the sound of water crashing against the ground made her love flow. The spacious home had always seemed cold to him after Queen left. It never really seemed like home without her being there with him.

The smooth sounds of trumpets soothed his soul. Bless began to sway back and forth, enjoying the moment, as an unexpected bell chimed. He instantly shot his eyes toward his door. *Who is that?* He never had guests, so he wasn't expecting anyone. Bless was confused as he set his drink down and made his way to the front door.

He opened the door, and to his surprise, a complete stranger was standing on his doorstep. It was a young lady who looked to be no older than 25 years of age. The rain was pouring down, and she was completely soaked. He looked into the woman's face in confusion, wondering if she was at the wrong house, because he had never seen her a day in his life.

She had kind, big brown welcoming eyes, and her hair was soaked and stringy. Her hair hung past her shoulders. The young lady had a bundle in her arms, what sounded like a screaming baby. She had it wrapped loosely in a pink blanket. She rocked her baby as she whispered to it, trying to keep it calm. She tried her best to cover the baby's face from the rain as she rocked it, trying to keep it calm. The loud crying sounded as if the baby was in pain, and it immediately tugged at Bless's heart. A child was something that Queen had always wanted, so he thought of her instantly.

"Hello, sir. So sorry to bother you, but my car broke down just up the road. My phone is dead, and I didn't know what to do," she said as tears filled her eyes.

"Sure. Sure. Come in, sweetheart," Bless said as he instantly wanted to help. His heart couldn't let him leave a crying baby and a distressed woman outside in the thunder and rain. He looked at her frame, noticed that she had a similar build to his Queen, and immediately thought about grabbing an old hoodie for her. "Let me grab my phone for you. Also, my wife was about your size. Let me see if I can find you some dry clothes."

"Bless your heart. God is good. Thank you so much," the woman said as she continued to rock the baby, trying her best to keep it calm. However, the crying just got louder and more frantic. "I'm sorry. She's terrified," the woman said as she looked down at the baby and whispered to it again.

Bless turned around to head to his coffee table, where his phone was. "It's okay. You can use my phone to call who you need while—" Bless said as he headed to the next room, but he was stopped mid-sentence when an iron bar crashed against the back of his head.

Bless fell forward and lost consciousness before he even hit the ground. He was out cold. A man with a bright skin tone and multiple scars on his face stood above him. He had sneaked in right behind the woman when Bless turned his back.

"Let's get it," the man said as he looked back at the woman, whose face, once innocent, now had a sinister look on it. She dropped the blanket that was in her hand, letting her bundle of joy drop on the ground. The sinister woman smiled as she carelessly dropped the small speaker box that was wrapped up. The recording of the baby crying sounded through the speaker box even louder now that it was exposed.

"Turn that bullshit off. Grab the ropes from outside. Let's get this nigga tied up before he wakes up," the man said as he dropped the crowbar and began to scan the house.

"I'm on it, daddy," the woman said as she quickly did as she was told. Bless had let the devil in, and that was when the game began.

Chapter One

Bless woke up groggily and in a compromising position. He was sitting upright in a chair, and his hands were bound by rope, tied behind his back. He realized that he was in his own living room, and he tried to make sense of what had gotten him there. The last thing Bless remembered was answering the door. The back of his head throbbed, and when he saw the unfamiliar man standing in front of him, he looked at him in confusion.

The fair-skinned intruder was light bright and seemed to be the next step above albino. His eyes had red circles around them, and his lips were so pink that it looked as if he had a touch of lipstick on them. This was an unusual-looking man. He had a weathered face. Scars were all over his cheeks and forehead as if he came directly out of a comic book. He definitely looked like a villain, the evilest type.

"What's going on? Why am I tied up?" Bless asked with a shaking voice. Fear was obviously present inside of him. It was all in his demeanor and tone.

"Rise and shine, sweetheart," the man said sarcastically. He circled around Bless and examined him carefully. He smiled and noticed that Bless was just as his partner described him: a four-eyed, soft-spoken man. An easy target to say the least.

"I think you might have made a mistake," Bless pleaded.

"No, we have the right house. Believe that," the man said as he began to look around the house and admire the paintings on the wall.

Bless looked confused as he sat there. While bound to a chair, Bless looked around and tried to get a grasp on who was in his home. He looked at the young lady who originally had been at his front door asking for help. She was now sitting on his counter, eating from a bag of potato chips as if she didn't have a care in the world.

The man stopped directly in front of Bless and looked down on him. "I'm not even going to play with you, my nigga. We know what's going on, and you do too. This is a stick-up. We came for the paper," Red said with confidence as he rubbed both of his hands together. He had a stern look in his eyes, and Bless stared directly into them. Bless felt like he was looking the devil directly in the face. The man didn't blink once, and he had a look of not giving a fuck. Bless instantly knew that the man didn't have it all and was legit crazy. It was written all over his face.

"A stick-up? Paper?" Bless asked while frowning up at him.

The man grew enraged. He was not in the mood to play games. He gave Bless a swift and powerful punch to his midsection. Bless folded over like a lawn chair as he let out a grunt from the thunderous blow.

"Okay, let's try this thing again," the man said as he aggressively placed his hand on the back of Bless's neck and pulled him slightly. He kneeled down so they could be face-to-face. The man wanted Bless to look directly into his eyes and see that he wasn't playing any types of games. He wanted to be firm and clear in his intentions.

"I'm going to be blunt with you," the man said as he intensely gazed at Bless. Without breaking eye contact with Bless, the man reached out his hand and wiggled his fingers, signaling his woman to hand him the gun. The woman hopped off of the counter and grabbed the gun from the countertop. She quickly walked it over to her man and placed it in his hand. The man, in a single sweeping motion, placed the pistol directly against Bless's forehead. The cold steel against his skin made Bless realize that it was a real situation.

"Okay, I get it. Please don't hurt me," Bless conceded.

"Now we are getting somewhere," the man responded while smiling. He stood up, but not before pushing Bless's head forcefully, causing him to jerk back violently. "I know that you have that delivery this evening, and I need that bag. Understand me?" Red instructed.

Bless instantly dropped his head in defeat, knowing that he had gotten caught slipping. "Damn, man," Bless whispered to himself as he shook his head in disbelief. He had moved so cautiously and low-key. He'd crossed all his t's and dotted his i's. How had this happened?

"I know, right? It's kinda fucked up, playboy," the man said playfully as he slowly began to circle Bless again. "You opened your door to a woman in distress and a crying baby and got much more. Life is fucked up, man. Tell me about it! I know more than anyone how cold this world can be. But dig this: I don't even want to kill you, my nigga. I just need that paper," the man said.

"It's not coming tonight," Bless admitted as he avoided eye contact with Red.

"What the fuck did you just say?" the man quizzed as he grabbed the back of Bless's neck again.

"I said it's not coming tonight. My mule got stuck in Denver on a layover. He won't be here until tomorrow night," Bless admitted.

"Don't fucking play with me!" the man yelled as the frustration began to set in.

"I'm telling the truth. He texted me about an hour ago, letting me know that his plane was delayed. Check my phone and verify it. It's right in the messages. My phone is on the coffee table," Bless said as he nodded in that direction.

The man immediately grabbed for Bless's phone. He began to go through the message threads. The most recent message was from Watson. The man instantly clicked on the name. He knew the name because of the intel he'd gotten on his mark. Watson was the money man and the person who delivered the cash to Bless. He read the message, and it confirmed what Bless had alleged. Watson had informed him that he would be over the following night when his new flight landed in Detroit.

"Fuck!" the man yelled in frustration as reality set in.

"What, baby?" the woman said as she hopped off the counter and walked over to her man, whose eyes were fixated on the message. The man showed her the message on the phone, and her joy seemed to be taken as well.

"Well, what are we going to do, Red?" she asked, panicking.

"Bitch, what did you just say?" Red harshly whispered as he wrapped his free hand around her neck. The woman put her hands up, conceding, as she gasped for air. Red was squeezing her neck so hard that it blocked her airway and veins began to form on her temples and forehead. He lifted her up, and she stood on her tiptoes as he looked at her with disgust. "You said my name. You birdbrain bitch."

"I'm sorry. I'm sorry," she managed to whisper, knowing that she had slipped up and made a big mistake by saying his name.

Red slightly eased up on his grasp and released her, letting her fall to the ground. She held her neck and coughed violently as she tried to catch her breath.

"Dumbass," Red said as he shook his head in disbelief while looking down at her beneath him. Bless just looked on, feeling sorry for the woman. Red refocused his attention on Bless.

"Well, it looks like we are going to be here for a while. Ain't that right, *Shawna?*" Red said, making sure her name was yelled out in the open as well. He didn't care either way at that point, because he had already made a decision to kill Bless after they got the money.

Red knelt down and rubbed Shawna's hair away from her face, exposing her wet cheeks. "Sorry, baby," he whispered in her ear as he cradled the back of her neck and awkwardly kissed her. "You just have to be smarter, okay?" Red instructed. Shawana nodded her head in agreement as her tears were still flowing, making her mascara streak down her face.

"Well, sir! I guess we are going to have a little sleepover. Time to get comfortable," Red said with a demented facial expression. He was going to wait until the money got there, and then he would murder Bless. Red's mind was set.

Chapter Two

A man in his late twenties sat patiently in a mint-condition vehicle. He looked around in awe, admiring his surroundings. He gripped the woodgrain circle that was in front of him and tightened his grip on the mint leather. He slowly cracked a smile as he stared at the world-renowned symbol that rested square in the middle of the steering wheel. He couldn't believe that he was in the driver's seat of a Bentley, the same car he used to dream about having while staring at a cutout of it on a cement wall. Just a few months prior, he was sitting in a federal penitentiary in the Upper Peninsula of Michigan. He shook his head in disbelief as he checked his rearview mirror. He saw the sign that read ARRIVALS as he sat curbside at Detroit Metropolitan Airport.

"One day. One day," the man said to himself under his breath as he imagined whipping the vehicle through his old neighborhood. He slowly traced the outside of the steering wheel with his right hand. He was determined that soon he would enjoy it as an owner rather than in his current position as a chauffeur.

Luck had been on his side, as he'd gotten the great job through a work-release program. Initially, Fonz wanted to return to the street game so he could get back on his feet, but instead, Fonz felt it was a blessing sent from above to steer him in the right direction. Fonz vowed to fly straight for as long as he could, and this route seemed to be the best option. Also, he loved the position's perks.

It wasn't bad for an alternative to a life of crime. The job was simple: every other Sunday he picked up his boss and took him to the airport. Then twelve hours later, he picked him back up to return him home. The best part of the job was that it paid in cash, which was helpful because between Fonz's three kids and their two mothers, child support drained any check that came through his pipeline. Not to mention he had an ill mother he cared for.

Fonz was working the current gig along with a third-shift job as a security guard. It didn't pay much, but he was doing the best he could with the opportunities placed in front of him. It was a far cry from his past life, and he'd switched his lifestyle tremendously since he'd been out. No matter how hard Fonz tried to convince himself that he could get used to living below the poverty line, he knew that it wouldn't last long. He'd been accustomed to having money since his early teenage years, and his current situation wasn't cutting it for him. Fonz needed more.

Alfonzo Coolidge was the name of the driver, but in the streets, he went by the moniker Fonz. He was an ex-convict who had a reputation for robbery. He was pretty good at it, too. As far as he was concerned, he would have never gotten caught if it weren't for him taking on a partner who eventually snitched on him and landed him in front of a judge. He spent six years in jail for a simple in-and-out job at a local check-cashing joint. Fonz vowed to never go back.

Fonz checked his wristwatch and then looked over to his right. He focused on the double doors, looking for his client to emerge from the airport. Just like clockwork, his client came walking out of the building.

A tall, lean, dark man with a cell phone to his ear headed toward the car. He looked to be in his mid-to-late thirties and wore a shiny bald head. The man wore a well-tailored charcoal suit, looking as if he'd stepped off the pages of the latest *GQ* magazine. His perfectly straight white teeth sparkled as he moved his mouth while talking on the phone. They seemed even brighter against his deep-chocolate complexion. The man wore reading glasses, and his posture didn't match his appearance. He walked with a sense of insecurity and seemed to be an introverted soul, avoiding eye contact with people as he maneuvered through the sea of travelers. The man walked with certain bashfulness that screamed "insecure." He carried a leather briefcase and swiftly made his way over to the car after spotting it on the curb.

Fonz noticed Mr. Brigante awkwardly weaving through the crowd and making his way over to the car. Fonz quickly checked his mirror to give himself a glance over, and he straightened his tie. He pulled up his collar, trying to hide his big neck tattoo that read "Linwood," paying homage to his neighborhood in the inner city of Detroit. Fonz quickly exited the car and made his way over to the passenger side, reaching for the handle. He opened the rear door, timing it perfectly with his boss's stride.

Mr. Brigante ducked his head and slid in smoothly, never breaking stride or even acknowledging Fonz. Fonz closed the door behind him and quickly made his way back into the driver seat. Not wanting to interrupt his boss's conversation, Fonz nodded to greet him. Mr. Brigante nonchalantly waved his hand as he continued his business call. Fonz strapped on his seat belt and merged into the lane heading out of the airport.

Fonz listened closely as he always did as the man discussed his business, hoping he could learn something in the midst of eavesdropping. Fonz always wondered what the hell his boss was involved in. He knew that it was something illegal, just because of the fact that the boss always dealt in cash and moved with a certain mystique. He didn't peg him as a drug dealer. He was much too timid for that. However, he did get the referral from a known drug dealer, and he knew that birds of a feather usually flocked together.

Maybe he sells black-market organs or funds illegal heists. What type of time is this nigga on? Fonz thought as he merged onto the freeway. For months, Fonz had wondered what line of work his boss was in, but he never had the balls to spark up a conversation to dig deeper. The one thing Fonz knew for certain was it was something that he wanted to keep from the government, which, nine times out of ten, meant an illegal endeavor. No one knew too much about his boss.

"These art units were beautiful. Not one flaw in them. They will sell quickly for sure. The flakes in the picture looked like fish scales," Mr. Brigante said to the other person on the phone.

Fonz listened closely and smirked slightly, knowing that Mr. Brigante was speaking in code. Fonz was much too slick for that disguised lingo to go over his head. To the untrained ear, one would think Mr. Brigante was talking about a painting. However, the way Fonz heard it, he was describing a batch of drugs coming in, hence the code word "units." Also, Fonz heard him say there were "no flaws," which wasn't referring to actual flaws. He was referring to the units being pure and not stepped on. *Who does this nigga think I am? An amateur? I can decipher homie's whole convo,* he thought while continuing to listen closely.

"Great, so once it's done, text me the final number. Good job, Watson. See you tomorrow evening," Mr. Brigante said just before he ended the phone call and focused on Fonz. "It's Alfonzo, right?"

"Uh, yes, Mr. Brigante," Fonz said, not expecting him to talk to him.

"Mr. Brigante is my father. Call me Bless," he said as he smiled and loosened his tie.

"Bless?" Fonz asked, making sure he'd heard it right.

"Yeah, I know. It's uncommon, right? My mom had a vivid imagination. She always said there's power in one's name, so she decided to name me Bless," he said, cracking a small smile.

"Well, sir, if you don't mind me saying, she was telling the truth. You are definitely blessed," Fonz said as he rubbed the dashboard in appreciation.

Bless chuckled lightly. "You can say that, I guess. Moms always know best," Bless said as he unbuttoned his cuff links, getting more comfortable. Bless stared at Fonz for a second and then began to speak again. "What about your mom? Is she still living?" he asked.

"Yeah, she's a trooper. She's battling cancer and taking it day by day," Fonz replied.

"Sorry to hear that. Do you see her a lot?" Bless questioned.

"I work two jobs, and I try to get over there to take care of her as much as I can. The plan is to save up enough to eventually get her a nurse a few times out of the week. Ya know, to help her out a bit while I'm away," Fonz said.

"I lost someone special to me not too long ago. It's tough. You should spend as much time as you can with her, because time is the only thing you can't get back. It's the most valuable thing on this earth," Bless said as he looked forward as if he was staring into space, not particularly looking at anything.

Fonz nodded in agreement but didn't respond. He appreciated the advice, knowing that Bless was telling the truth. Fonz wanted to keep the conversation going because he had never said more than two words to him during the three months that he had worked for him. He wanted to figure out what exactly Bless did for a living. The mystery was killing him, and since the ice was broken, he thought that was his way in.

"So, what line of work are you in?" Fonz asked as he checked his mirror and switched lanes.

"I'm a painter and an art dealer," Bless responded.

"Business must be good," Fonz said as he cracked a smile involuntarily.

"It's booming," Bless said with a smirk. He looked at Fonz, and they made eye contact through the rearview mirror. Fonz knew at that moment that Bless was into some illegal shit. Fonz had doubts before, but he knew a criminal grin when he saw one. Fonz nodded, knowing nothing more needed to be said.

"Turn that up for me please," Bless said as the faint sounds of jazz pumped through the speakers. Fonz quickly dialed up the music and continued to cruise down Interstate 75, heading to the quiet, secluded suburbs of Auburn Hills. Fonz remained quiet the rest of the way to Bless's residence. However, his mind unremittingly began to churn. He had been raised in the streets where the prized position was either a plug or a wealthy target. Either way, Fonz wanted to learn more.

A half hour later, the luxury car was pulling into the long driveway that led to the extravagant home. Just as usual, a modest Honda Accord was sitting there, parked. It was Fonz's mom's car and what he was using to get around until he got on his feet. He always parked his car there and switched cars before coming to pick up Bless. When Fonz parked, he quickly hopped out and skipped over to the back passenger side to open the door for Bless. Bless stepped out and nodded to Fonz before picking up his ringing cell phone. Fonz closed the door behind him, and his mind was running 1,000 miles per minute. He wanted to take advantage of the opportunity to build with Bless, so he went for it.

"Excuse me," Fonz said as he held one finger up, trying to catch Bless's attention.

Bless, still engaged in his phone conversation, turned slightly and looked at Fonz to see what he wanted.

"Sorry to bother you, but may I use the restroom?" Fonz requested, trying to gain access to Bless's home as an attempt to get in good with him.

Bless paused as if he was thinking hard about it and then nodded in agreement. "Sure, I guess. Come on in," Bless said as he headed to the door.

Fonz quickly closed the door and followed Bless up the walkway. Fonz didn't show it physically, but he was beaming on the inside. He could spot people like Bless from a mile away. He was the brains behind an operation, but he had no street in him. In a world of sharks, Bless was something that you called food. Fonz could tell Bless didn't have any toughness. It was all in his demeanor. Bless lacked self-confidence, which usually meant a man was weak.

Fonz admired the property's immaculate landscaping as he followed close behind. He watched closely as Bless approached the door. Rather than pull out a set of house keys, Bless placed a thumb on a sensor and held it there for a second. Then the sounds of a few deadbolts clicking erupted. Bless ended his phone conversation and pushed the big steel door open.

Fonz was amazed at the technology. It was something that he had never witnessed before. The sophisticated entry method blew his mind, and Fonz watched as he stepped over the threshold, entering the home. Marble floors lined the home, and a gush of cool air hit Fonz's face as he trailed behind Bless. The smell of lavender filled his nostrils, and Bless stepped to the side to give Fonz a pathway to walk.

"The bathroom is down the hall and to the right," Bless said as he looked at Fonz skeptically.

"Thanks," Fonz responded as he walked down the long corridor and admired a remarkable painting that lined the wall. The abundance of radiant colors and abstract objects were stunning to the naked eye. The lights had a trickle effect, so with each step he took, a new area of the hall would light up. Fonz looked around in disbelief as the seemingly futuristic home amazed him. He spotted the bathroom to the right and stepped in.

Bless took off his suit jacket and got settled into his home. He walked into his marble kitchen and set his briefcase on top of the counter. He then rested his hands on the sink and took a deep breath. He looked over at the life-sized, hand-painted portrait of his wife and smiled, admiring her beauty. The smile instantly turned into grief as he closed his eyes, remembering the only true love of his life.

Queen sat naked in the chair. Her shoulders were pulled back, and her posture was immaculate. Her body glowed radiantly as her smooth cocoa complexion was on full display. Her big, long legs were crossed, and her extra serving of loveliness was hanging over the sides of the stool. Queen wasn't a small lady of any sorts, but she was well put together. The smooth baby skin of her plump body was moisturized with natural oils, and it was as if she were shining. Her sides had small rolls where her ribs were, and her wide hips were on full display. She slowly bopped her foot to the smooth music as Badu played in the background.

The smell of sage burned throughout the home, mixed with the scent of marijuana. Queen subtly took a pull of the joint as she bopped her head to the music. Her breasts were perky, sitting high, and her full, dark areolas were on exhibit. Her natural hair was wrapped in a multicolored head wrap, and only the soft baby hairs that rested on the edge of her scalp were visible.

Queen smiled as she caught the eyes of her man studying her intensely. Bless's piercing stare had extreme passion and admiration as he crossed his arms, squinting his eyes. He was covered in paint and was shirtless with snug-fitting khakis. Different specks of paint were all over his body from his hours of creating different shades, trying desperately to recreate Queen's honey brown complexion. He stood barefoot in the middle of his garage with his paintbrush in his hand. He was painting what he considered one of his most important pieces ever.

"I'm almost finished, my love. Thanks for being patient with me," he said in a low baritone voice.

"Patience is mandatory when you're in love with a man. What would I ever rush anything for? We have an entire lifetime to experience together. Patience is—"

"A virtue," Bless cut in, finishing her sentence as he stood before her, examining her facial features. Bless froze as he looked into her big brown eyes, and the urge to cry overcame him. His soul was connected to hers, and there was no mistaking that. He understood that a love like hers came once in a lifetime, and that alone gave him tears of joy every time he thought about it. She was gentle. She was kind. She was patient. Most importantly, she was his woman. They had been together since they were teenagers.

Queen put the marijuana-filled joint to her lips, taking a deep pull of smoke into her lungs. Then she slowly puckered her lips and blew out a stream of creamy smoke. The smoke drifted into Bless's face as he squinted and smoothly turned his head.

"I'm sorry, daddy," Queen said while smirking at his cuteness. She rubbed the side of his face and giggled.

She frequently blew trees to relax and get herself into a familiar vibe. However, she felt guilty knowing that Bless wasn't a smoker. "I'm going to stop smoking one day," she said. She watched as he turned back to her with a small grin.

"No worries. Do what makes you happy, love. Everyone has an addiction. Mine just happens to be you." Bless stated it with sincerity while he stared at her in admiration. He leaned in and kissed her deep right dimple, slowly moved to her left dimple, and followed it with a gentle kiss to her forehead. Bless held the kiss on her forehead and whispered, "My pretty girl."

That move of his always sent sparks through her spine. It never failed. While most men thought that women had a cord connecting their clitoris to their heart, the real "hot spot" was their foreheads. That's where women truly felt the love. For that is the spot where women usually experience their first kisses. A parent usually shows their love to an infant by kissing them on their forehead. It is subconsciously embedded in a woman's anatomy to feel real love by this type of kiss. Only a man who paid attention to detail understood this.

Queen closed her eyes and swayed back and forth as if music began to play. There was no music playing—the Badu had ended—but their vibration was real and on the same accord. She could feel it moving her.

"I love you," she whispered.

"I love you too, pretty girl," he responded as he stepped back and went directly to his large canvas that was mounted on the wall. He began to swiftly stroke his paintbrush, and he continued crafting his chocolate Mona Lisa.

Fonz exited the bathroom and headed down the corridor to the kitchen area where Bless was. The hallway's walls were full of paintings, and splashes of red were throughout each one. Fonz looked closely and admired the works of art. The attention to detail was stellar, and all of them were outlined by thick cedar-oak frames. The high ceilings in the house seemed to make his footsteps echo even louder throughout the quiet home.

The technology blew his mind as Fonz once again looked down at the floors lighting up with each new step. He studied each painting as he went past them and began to notice a recurring theme in each one. They all had a fox as the main focal point. Fonz even saw a painting that had a man posing in a suit, however, his head was that of a fox. Every painting was different with the fox being the common denominator. Surprisingly, the fox made it all come together. The color clashes and intricate palettes were visually stunning. *This looks amazing!* Fonz thought as he looked on in admiration.

He reached the kitchen and saw that Bless had taken off his shirt and only had a beater on. He was already engaged in painting when Fonz walked in.

"Uh, thanks for letting me use your restroom, sir," Fonz said as he walked up on him. Bless was so locked in on his painting that he didn't even look back at Fonz. Fonz stood there awkwardly and waited to see if Bless was going to acknowledge him, but he didn't. Bless was beginning to paint on the canvas that was propped on the wall. "I'll just let myself out," Fonz said unsurely.

"Sorry about that. I didn't want to lose this vision I had for my new piece," Bless said as he used his index finger to balance his glasses on the brim of his nose. He then set the paint brush down and wiped his hands on a towel that lay nearby. "You want a beer?" Bless hesitantly asked as he walked over to the refrigerator and opened the door.

"Hell yeah," Fonz said. He couldn't control his eagerness, and the words just seemed to slip out of his mouth.

"Great." Bless pulled out two longneck bottles. "Here ya go," Bless said. He tossed one over, and Fonz quickly caught it. Bless popped open the bottle and began making his way over to where Fonz was standing.

"Cheers," Bless said as he raised his bottle and pointed at Fonz. Fonz then popped his open and followed suit, clinking his bottle's neck with Bless's.

Clink!

Both men took a swallow, and Fonz began to nod his head in approval at the taste. "This is some good stuff," Fonz said as he examined the foreign-looking bottle.

"Yeah. It's Irish beer. I get it shipped directly to me. Only kind of beer I drink," Bless said, smiling as he took another swallow. "You play chess?" Bless asked as he threw his head in the direction of the table that was off in the corner.

"Chess? Hell yeah, I can play a little," Fonz said as he nodded his head. Fonz's gamble had worked, and he had gotten Bless to open up a bit. Fonz knew that he was one step closer to seeing exactly what type of business Bless was in. He knew that selling those paintings had not gotten him the house and the lifestyle that he was living. Fonz was determined to find out Bless's game. Fonz didn't know exactly how, but he did know one thing: he wanted in.

"This is a nice-ass house, bruh. The floors, the lights, everything is so futuristic. Some real fly shit," Fonz said as he looked around.

"Thanks. I love new technology. I have the most modern systems installed throughout the house," Bless answered.

They sat down and began to play. Fonz watched the man across from him closely, trying to figure him out. Bless's timid nature and the way his shoulders would always hunch over were dead giveaways of his meekness. As they played, Fonz noticed that Bless would occasionally check his phone as if he was waiting for something. Fonz tried to eye hustle and see what was on his screen, but he couldn't get a good look from where he was sitting across the table.

Bless studied the board strategically and remained quiet as he made his moves against Fonz. It was obvious that Bless was much more advanced than Fonz as he quickly removed his pieces from the board, knocking them off one by one.

"I'm kind of rusty. Haven't played since I been home from upstate," Fonz said shamefully as he moved his queen piece across the board.

"I can see that," Bless said calmly as he looked at his phone again. A text had just come through. He slightly grinned and then set his phone down. He refocused on the board and then looked up at Fonz. Bless used his index finger to prop his glasses up on the bridge of his nose and smiled nervously. "Check," Bless said.

"Damn," Fonz said as he studied the board, seeing that he had no way out. He was trapped. He knew the game was about to be over.

"See? You play fast and without a plan. Chess is a thinking man's game," Bless stated.

"You got me. You got me," Fonz admitted as he pretended like he cared. However, inside his mind, chess was the last thing Fonz was thinking of. He didn't give a fuck about the game they were playing. He just was trying to make a connection, so if losing a few chess games helped Fonz do that, he was all for it.

"You're not so bad. You just rush. I can see it all in your game. I was baiting you with every step," Bless said in a matter-of-fact tone.

"Baiting?" Fonz asked, trying to understand what Bless was talking about.

"Yeah, bait. One of the laws of power is 'use bait if necessary.' This works well in chess, too. I did it on you all game," Bless said, breaking down his tactics for Fonz to clearly understand. Bless's phone buzzed, and he glanced at it and nodded his head in approval.

"Checkmate," Bless said, as he took down Fonz's king. He then looked at Fonz, smiled, and took the last swallow of his beer. "Give me a sec. I have to take a leak," Bless said as he stood up and hurried to the back of the house where the bathroom was located.

Fonz stared at the board and saw that he really had no chance of winning that game. Bless had trapped his king from all angles.

Fonz noticed that Bless's phone was still on the table. It just so happened that it began to buzz as Fonz was looking at it. Fonz looked across the room and made sure that Bless was nowhere in sight and then quickly grabbed it. He looked at the text message that was across the screen, and it was a message from a person named Watson. Fonz immediately knew it was the person he was speaking to on the phone earlier. The message read: 350K. I'll be by tonight to drop off. Talk soon.

Fonz heard the footsteps of Bless returning and quickly put the phone back in its original position on the table. Bless returned while drying his hands on his shirt.

"Another game?" Bless asked as he sat back down at the table.

"I wish. I got a call from my mother while you were away. I have to go check on her. She isn't feeling too well," Fonz lied as he abruptly stood.

"Oh, yeah. Okay. Take care of your mother for sure," Bless said as he stood up and reached out to shake Fonz's hand.

"No doubt. Thanks for the beer, homie," Fonz said with a fake smile.

"Maybe we can play again soon. You know, I don't have too many friends, so a good game does good for my mental, ya know?" Bless said as he awkwardly shook Fonz's hand.

Fonz nodded his head in agreement and cringed on the inside, knowing that Bless was not his type of company. Fonz couldn't imagine becoming friends with a square like him. Fonz would much rather rob Bless. And from what Fonz just saw, he knew that there was a very high probability of that happening in the near future.

The seed was planted and the greed consumed Fonz's thoughts. He wanted to take what Bless had, and his mind had already been set. Fonz was about to put a play down on his boss. He saw a sucker in Bless, so he was about to hit the lick. Fonz had been waiting for a moment like this since he got out. He was searching for a plan or a sense of where he was going. Fonz had finally gotten that. He had a plan. It had been a long time coming.

Let's take a stroll down memory lane to see how Fonz got to this point.

Chapter Three

Every day that passed, Fonz vowed to do something, anything, toward bettering himself. His goal was to make sure he would need as little help as possible transitioning back into society the day he was released. He didn't want to spend months or even weeks completing rehabilitation programs or work-release requirements. Fonz had to be honest with himself. The longer it took him to make money and establish himself, the higher the probability that he would end up right back in the game, surviving by living a life of crime and eventually ending up back in the system.

Prison is a horrible place. It is a cement box where souls are snatched away and held hostage by the prison guards and other inmates. During the day, blind eyes watch over the cell blocks, often ignoring issues that should be addressed for selfish motives. Just as many underhanded actions and crime take place in each facility as they do on the streets, regardless of the security level. At night, horrifying screams and pleas for help echo through the air, putting a smile on the faces of the heartless and instant fear in the hearts of those who are deemed weaker flesh. They live daily with paranoid thoughts of being next on the list of doomed souls.

Fonz knew right away the prison life was not the life for him. With his well-established reputation and respect in the streets, Fonz had allies in prison upon his arrival. Safety was never a concern. However, the temptation of becoming more corrupt and caught up in the game deeper was an ever-present battle.

Fonz landed residency in the Upper Peninsula facility after getting caught up in a string of robberies that the police were able to eventually tie together. Robbery was his game, and he was phenomenal at it. Fonz was schooled by some of the legends in his neighborhood when he was a mere 14 years old. It wasn't long before he took what he had learned and added his own twist, taking the craft to the next level.

As superb as he was, Fonz always seemed to fall short due to his desire to impress the multiple women in his life. He allowed his bad habit to cloud his judgment. He sometimes rushed selling the items he retrieved from jobs to get quick money instead of its full value for the sole purpose of blowing it on the ladies. He engaged in pillow talk extensively, many times sharing things that should have gone to the grave with him. Ultimately, his addiction to gaining attention from his female admirers was what landed him in prison for six years, three months, two weeks, and sixteen days.

After three weeks of research, surveillance, and careful planning, Fonz and one of his neighborhood mentors developed and executed a plan to rob the members of a very exclusive poker club, one by one. Everything was going excellent. Fonz decided to take one of his top three favorite beauties, Lolita, on a romantic weekend getaway. On their last night together, Fonz began to tell Lolita how he got the money to fund their trip and promised her that if she stayed loyal by his side, there would be much more to come in the future.

"It's simple, baby," Fonz began to explain as he took a puff from the half-smoked blunt in his fingers. "We learned about this exclusive poker club and found out the days they have games. One by one we followed the dudes. We followed them to their houses, their jobs, hell, one guy we even followed to his secret boyfriend's house." Fonz and Lolita both laughed at what was said.

"Boyfriend?" Lolita asked, still laughing.

Fonz nodded his head. "Yes. His boyfriend," he responded. "After that, everything else was simple. We got a four-man crew together and created a thorough schedule and started hitting them niggas' cribs one by one. We've been getting so much shit, and we've only done three spots so far."

Intrigued by everything Fonz was telling her, Lolita started putting together a couple of plans of her own. One was to guarantee that Fonz trusted her completely. The other plan was to get a piece of the profit that was coming from the robberies. The gifts and trips that Fonz had given her just weren't enough. She craved more. She knew exactly how to get Fonz to listen to her and how to make him say yes to just about anything she asked.

"I appreciate you so much. Nobody has ever done anything like this for me before, baby. You know how to make a girl feel special," Lolita whispered in Fonz's ear as she slowly placed soft, moist kisses on his face and neck.

"Anything for you, boo. I just want to put a smile on your face," said Fonz with his eyes closed and arms spread wide on the bed.

Lolita could feel Fonz's body relaxing and his penis growing, getting harder and harder. She continued to strategically place kisses all over his body while sliding down his boxers. Fonz was so focused on the tingling sensation traveling all over his body, he didn't realize that he was now lying in the bed completely naked. Once Lolita reached his throbbing manhood, she slowly started licking the head while stroking up and down his shaft with her hand.

Fonz was under her spell the moment he felt the heat from her breath on his tip. As she began to take him in her mouth more and more, he couldn't help but to express his excitement by yelling, "Shiiiit!"

Lolita smiled on the inside. His cries of pleasure were all she needed to confirm that her plan was coming together perfectly. She continued to do tricks with her tongue and mouth, making Fonz tense up and squirm.

"Daddy, I have something I want to talk to you about," Lolita said in between sucks and slurps.

"Huh? What?" Fonz asked in a cloud of confusion and pleasure.

"I need you to hear me out about something. It's important," continued Lolita.

"Do we have to talk about this now? I mean, I want to help you, baby, but can it wait until you're done?" Fonz pleaded.

Lolita smiled. "You promise we'll talk about it?"

"Yes! I promise," Fonz assured her as he pushed her head back down.

Without hesitation, Lolita took all of Fonz's ten inches in her mouth and pushed it as far as she could down her throat. She gagged and slurped on his dick until she felt the warmth from his cum on the back of her tongue.

"Gooootttt dammmnnn!" Fonz screamed as he grabbed the back of Lolita's head in pleasure.

After the two cleaned up and were back in bed relaxing, Lolita went right into what Fonz agreed to do. She began to explain how she could be an asset to his operation. Lolita shared that, due to her upbringing, she gained knowledge from a fashionista and a social-elite consultant. Her mom had worked as a housekeeper for a very prominent family in Bloomfield Township, Michigan, since Lolita was 8 years old. Growing up around the wealthy exposed her to a lot of new experiences. The couple had all boys and no girls, so the wife took a liking to Lolita. She would take Lolita out to shop at extravagant boutiques and have brunch at country clubs, and she taught Lolita everything she could. Lolita knew all of the hottest designers and their worth. She had major skills, including being able to identify what items were knockoffs and what was the real thing. She was well versed and educated on different wines, cigars, art, and even the work of specific jewelers.

"I want in," expressed Lolita. "You need me."

Fonz smirked. "I need you?" he asked. "Now that's funny."

Lolita went on to further plead her case. She knew that, with her knowledge, she could make sure that the items they were stealing were actually worth something. She could make sure that they walked away with all profit and not a bunch of worthless junk.

Lolita's sales pitch had definitely caught Fonz's ear and attention. She was right. A little under half of the items they retrieved from their first jobs was junk. Even though they still walked away with a nice bag for each member of the crew, if there was a way to eliminate losing so much on each job, that could potentially double their profit.

"I mean, if you are going to take the risk, you need to make sure it's worth it. Right?" Lolita asked as she traced Fonz's chest with her fingertip.

"I don't know, baby. This can get really dangerous. I don't want anything to happen to you," Fonz said with uncertainty in his voice and on his face.

"Can you please just think about it? Better yet, let's just try it once. See how it goes. If you're still not comfortable with it, then I'll leave it alone and never ask you again," proposed Lolita.

In his gut, Fonz knew this probably was not a good look for the system and operation he had established.

Lolita had never done anything illegal a day in her life. Not even shoplifted a pack of candy before. She just wasn't that type of girl. Bringing her in on a full-blown robbery operation made no sense. Not on a job of this magnitude and risk. However, when it came to women, nothing Fonz ever did seemed to make sense.

He agreed to give it a try one time and go from there, as long as she made sure she followed three rules: (1) never be late for a hit, (2) never talk to anyone outside of the crew about anything, and (3) everything taken must be sold or destroyed. Keep nothing for yourself.

The first two hits that Fonz let Lolita tag along on went smoothly. Lolita had a good eye and quick hands. She cleaned out closets, jewelry boxes, wine collections, and more, only grabbing items that were authentic and high in value. Lolita was a pro! Fonz was impressed and glad he gave her a chance. That was until Lolita started to get comfortable and sloppy.

One night while out at dinner, Fonz noticed something on Lolita's wrist that looked very familiar. It was a Cartier Love Bracelet from one of their jobs. He remembered the bracelet due to its unique pink gold with multicolor-stone design. He grabbed Lolita's wrist and held it tight.

"What the fuck is this, Lolita?" he asked in a stern voice. "Are you crazy? You know the rules! Why do you still have this?"

Lolita looked at Fonz with a small amount of fear in her eyes. She would have been terrified if not for the fact that they were in public, and she knew Fonz would only go so far with his chastisement.

"Let go of my arm!" she hissed through clenched teeth. "It's just one bracelet. Don't get all sensitive and get your panties all in a bunch! What's the problem?"

It took all the resistance and self-control Fonz had in his body not to reach across the table and smack Lolita across the face. “Are you fucking stupid? What are the rules? Everything must go! You don’t keep anything. Especially some exclusive shit like this. Get rid of it. Tonight!” Fonz said, scolding Lolita.

“Why are you talking to me like I’m a kid? I know what I’m doing,” Lolita said as she finally was able to snatch her arm away from Fonz’s death grip. “No! I’m not getting rid of anything. It’s one freakin’ bracelet! I don’t run in the same circles with these people. Who’s going to see it? Relax!” Lolita snapped as she picked up her glass and took a sip of her wine.

Fonz was in disbelief at the words that came flowing out of Lolita’s mouth. She was caught up, and he knew what he had to do. He stood up out of his chair while reaching in his pocket and pulled out some cash. He threw the money on the table then bent over to whisper in Lolita’s ear.

“You smelling yourself I see. Talking real big for a little girl. You showed up to a job late last month, and I let it slide, let you off with a warning. That was my fault, and I should have nipped this setup then. Now you’re keeping shit? Wearing it like it’s something you bought for yourself? You’re too much of a risk.” Fonz stood up and fixed the jacket he was wearing. “That should be enough money on the table to cover the bill and get you an Uber home. You are officially out of the crew. We’re done.” Fonz turned and walked out of the restaurant.

Lolita was shaking with anger and frustration. Her emotional instability was beyond any level of emotion she had ever felt. The ugly feeling of rejection also began to set in, a feeling she had never faced. Lolita was frozen. Her mind was telling her to scream, to grab Fonz and not let him walk out. She couldn’t move an inch.

Lolita snapped out of her trance and immediately grabbed her phone. She tried calling Fonz, hoping that he was just teaching her a lesson and would answer the phone. It never happened. Her six text messages also went unanswered. Two hours passed, and she'd heard not one word from Fonz. Her bitter reality started to sink in. After finishing an entire bottle of wine, Lolita finally paid the bill for their dinner and left the restaurant.

Three weeks later, Fonz was in his apartment and lying on the couch watching TV. As he took a sip from the cup of Faygo Red Pop he'd just poured for himself, the hair on his arm started to stand up. Suddenly, there was tension in the air. It felt thick and heavy. Before Fonz could place his cup down on the round glass coffee table, a cavalry of police officers kicked in the door, guns drawn and pointing at him.

Somewhat shaken up, Fonz had enough experience and street smarts to fight through his nervousness and stay calm. The only thing that came from his mouth was, "I want to see my lawyer," as he was tackled to the floor and handcuffed. After the police ransacked every room, totally destroying his furniture and the entire apartment, Fonz was placed under arrest and read his rights.

He knew they didn't find anything in his spot that could be used against him. If nothing else, he was organized, careful, and never sloppy. However, they arrested him anyway. Something major was off the mark, and the pit of Fonz's stomach was telling him that things were about to get a lot worse.

As two officers walked Fonz through the door of the precinct, he took a quick glance around the room. It was a habit he picked up along the years as a part of his trade as a thief. As he slowly turned his head, he thought he saw a familiar face and quickly did a double take. Fonz could not believe his eyes. Sitting at a desk talking to a detective was Lolita. Tears were streaming down her face, and her lips trembled. Her eyes were puffy and red like she had been crying for hours. Fonz was engulfed with rage, glaring at Lolita with a look of death, hoping she would look up and see him. Then he noticed that Lolita was not being her normal animated self, partially because she was not moving her hands around as she talked. It was because she couldn't. Her hands were cuffed behind her back.

"When someone comes in voluntarily to snitch," Fonz murmured to himself, "they don't get handcuffed. What the hell is going on? Is Lolita under arrest or not?"

Fonz sat in an interrogation room for two and a half hours before his lawyer finally showed up. "Hello, Mr. Coolidge. How are you holding up?" asked a middle-aged Italian man in a black tailored suit. It was Fonz's attorney, P.W. Anderson.

"I'm about to lose my shit sitting in here. What the hell is taking so long?" Fonz answered. "Why am I here? What is going on?"

"To be honest with you, buddy, it's not looking good. Do you know a Lolita Franklin?"

Fonz just nodded his head up and down, signifying he knew her.

"Ms. Franklin was seen wearing a Cartier bracelet and carrying a limited-edition handbag of some sort while visiting her mother at work. The person who saw these items is a friend of her mother's employer. She claimed the items were taken when her house was burglarized a month ago. The victim reported what she saw to the police. Ms. Franklin's home was searched today, and more items from that robbery and a few others were found in her possession. . . ."

Every word Mr. Anderson spoke after that point fell on Fonz's deaf ears. He couldn't believe Lolita was hiding shit from the hits all along. Even after he told her to get rid of the bracelet, she still continued to wear it like it wasn't a big deal. And the worst part of it all was there was a strong possibility that she snitched on him.

"Just tell me this," interrupted Fonz. "Did she give me up? Is that why I'm in here?"

"Well, yes and no," Mr. Anderson explained. "Ms. Franklin also kept a ledger of everything that was done: every location, what was collected from each job, and what each person got. Your name was listed in the book. They matched the names in the ledger with the names in her cell phone, and the rest speaks for itself. Here we are. As far as I know, she is not cooperating and has asked to speak to an attorney, but that's not who you should be concerned with."

Fonz shook his head in disbelief and chuckled. "I guess common sense just isn't so common," he said to himself. Then the last statement his attorney said played back in his head. "Wait? What do you mean?" Fonz asked, puzzled by the comment.

"JC. That's the real problem. They matched his fingerprints to a check-cashing robbery last year and have offered him a deal if he talks. Talking is exactly what he's doing."

Fonz pounded his fists into the table. He was so busy watching Lolita that he never gave JC a second thought. Fonz and JC went way back. JC was one of the few street legends in the game who had never been to prison, and that was the main reason Fonz thought he could trust him. Turned out to be one of the biggest mistakes of his life.

Once cell phone records and other evidence were collected and presented, there was no turning back for Fonz and his fellow thieves. The evidence was so strong against them, there was no point in fighting the case until the end, allowing it to drag out in court. After months of going back and forth with the prosecutor, Fonz finally accepted a deal and received a sentence of four to fifteen years for both robberies. Lolita also took a plea and was sentenced to eighteen months in prison.

After being locked up for a little over a month, Fonz got a letter from Lolita. She apologized for everything that happened and for her carelessness. She knew if she had not been so stubborn and had followed the rules, they would have never been arrested, and JC would have never been in a position to turn on Fonz. Lolita expressed her love and respect for Fonz. He'd taught her so much about life and about herself. No matter what the future brought to either of them, he would always hold a special place in her heart.

As her letter came to an end, Fonz's eyes grew bigger and bigger as he read her closing words. He suddenly started to look clammy and flushed in his face. The letter fell from his fingers and gently landed on the floor of his cell. During the intake process, Lolita had passed out. She was taken to the prison's infirmary, where she was given a complete physical. To her surprise, Lolita was five months pregnant with Fonz's baby.

The day Fonz had been working so hard for had finally arrived. As he put pictures of his kids and personal items in a box provided by the prison, his stomach fluttered with butterflies and anticipation. Deep down inside his heart, Fonz was very proud of what he had accomplished during his time locked up. He completed his GED and earned an associate's degree in psychology from a community college, something he never even thought about before he got locked up. He also tutored other inmates and helped them learn how to read. His dedication to bettering himself and others caught the eye of one of his professors, Dr. Todd Williams. The two grew to be very close.

Dr. Williams taught abnormal psychology and cognitive behavioral psychology at the community college. He had a private practice and was a member of a prisoner reform coalition. Dr. Williams admired Fonz's heart. Although Fonz still possessed his rough street exterior, he was always willing to learn something new. His mentality had clearly evolved, and he was ready to be a different man. Dr. Williams mentored Fonz and groomed him professionally as well. He helped Fonz with his speech and diction, including building his vocabulary. He also taught Fonz basic societal norms and etiquette that most street guys had no clue about. When Dr. Williams found out that Fonz was given a release date, he used his connections on the reform coalition to get Fonz set up with a release sponsor: his colleague, Dr. Celeste Ose.

Dr. Ose was the director of the Building Connections Prison Reform Center. The center offered GED and high school diploma classes, résumé building, job-interview training, and trade-building skills. Dr. Williams trusted Dr. Ose. Her track record and reputation were impeccable. Very few of the inmates who successfully completed one of her programs returned to prison. With Fonz's potential, Dr. Williams knew he was a perfect fit for Dr. Ose's program.

"Hey, man. You ready?" asked the energetic Dr. Williams. He was in his mid-forties but didn't look a day over 30. His wire-framed glasses fit his face perfectly and were a great complement to his five o'clock shadow beard. Dr. Williams was a fair-skinned Puerto Rican. If it weren't for his accent, someone would definitely think he was a white man.

"What's up, man? Hell yeah, I'm ready!" joked Fonz. "What are you doing here? I thought I was meeting you outside."

Dr. Williams grinned. "You're not the only one with a little pull around here."

"Oh, okay. I see you," Fonz replied, laughing.

Fonz finished packing up his belongings and walked to the bars that were the front door of his cell. He gave his cellmate a handshake as the guard who'd escorted Dr. Williams yelled for the other guard to unlock the bars.

As Fonz stepped out of his cell, Dr. Williams saw the pictures of his children in his box. He reached in and pulled them out. "Are all these beautiful children yours?" asked Dr. Williams.

"Yeah, man," answered Fonz. "My princess and my three soldiers. Prince is fourteen, Khalil is eleven, Li'l Fonz is nine, and Dia'Mond is five. Dia'Mond's mom had her in prison. Thank God her grandmother was able to keep her and take care of her until her mom got out. I don't know how I would have made it if my baby had ended up in foster care. That would have been too much to take. I want better for my kids, you know."

Dr. Williams could see the pain in Fonz's face as he talked about his children. He didn't have any kids of his own, but it didn't stop him from empathizing with Fonz and his situation. "Wow. That's pretty heavy, man. What about your other kids? Are they in good situations?" Dr. Williams inquired.

"For the most part, yeah, they're good. Prince and Khalil live in Atlanta with their grandparents. Their mom got turned out by some white dude she met online when they were ten and eight years old. Craziest shit I've ever seen. I can remember when she used to cuss me out for smoking weed. Last I heard she was hooked on pills and powder, turning tricks at a truck stop. I wish they lived closer, but they have a great life down there. They're really blessed. I'm thankful." Fonz put his finger to the corner of his left eye to stop a tear from falling. He loved his children more than anything. It hurt him to know that when they needed him the most, he was in prison.

"Li'l Fonz stays with his mom, Elle, back in my hometown. Now his mother has my heart! I'm still in love with that girl. That's one of the first places I'm going when I get back to the city. I wish I could have married her," Fonz shared as he grinned from ear to ear.

Dr. Williams tried not to crack a smile, but failed. He knew that Fonz was trying to lighten the situation. He wasn't going to take that from him. "Maybe you still can. Never say never, my friend. Especially when it comes to matters of the heart," Dr. Williams encouraged Fonz.

Fonz shook his head. "Nah. Unfortunately that ship has sailed. She's engaged to one of the homies from the neighborhood."

"Wait. She started dating your friend? That's cold, brotha," responded Dr. Williams in shock.

"Not a friend. More like an associate. I can't be mad about it though. He's a real one. Much respect in the streets, and he takes good care of her and my son. I guess that's a piece of my karma for landing my black ass in this hellhole." Fonz reached in his box and handed Dr. Williams a picture of a caramel-complected woman with hazel almond-shaped eyes, a bright and wide smile, and a small diamond earring in her nose.

Dr. Williams seemed to be stuck in a daze at her beauty. "She's beautiful," he said.

"Yes. Yes, she is," agreed Fonz.

The two men finally made their way to the front of the prison. Correctional officers gave Fonz handshakes and nods of encouragement as he passed through each secure area. Once he reached the final set of doors, the warden of the prison stepped out. He shook Fonz's and Dr. Williams's hands and ordered the guards to open the gates. Fonz walked out with his head held high, allowing the brisk air and sunlight to caress his face like old friends. The moment he had been working hard for had finally arrived.

Chapter Four

After Dr. Williams got Fonz checked in with his parole officer, he took Fonz to his mother's house. "I will be here at eight thirty a.m. sharp to take you to the center tomorrow. Please make sure you are presentable from head to toe. I've been bragging about you. Don't make me look bad," joked Dr. Williams with one eyebrow raised.

Fonz laughed hysterically. "Make you look bad? I think you have that already handled!"

Dr. Williams shook his head and motioned for Fonz to get out of his car. "Get some rest tonight," he instructed as Fonz closed the door of his silver C-Class Benz.

Fonz stood outside staring at the small brick house for at least two minutes. The house held so many memories of his life story. It was the house he'd grown up in. It was the house he'd lost his virginity in, the basement he'd hidden his first stash in. Fonz had to catch his emotions and keep himself from getting upset. When he moved out of this small brick home at the age of 18, he told himself he would never call it home again. But here he was, fresh out of prison and with no other options. Fonz vowed right then and there that this living situation would only be temporary. He could not be a grown-ass man living at home with his mother.

As Fonz's arm reached out to knock on the black metal screen door, the security door opened before he had a chance to actually knock. A slim, elderly woman with salt-and-pepper hair and an emerald green bathrobe on opened the door. She and Fonz stood there, emotions pouring over, staring at each other. It was obvious that the moment was surreal for both of them.

"M . . . Ma . . . Mama?" stuttered Fonz.

He did not recognize the frail brown-toned woman who stood in front of him. When he last saw his mother, she was about forty pounds heavier. Her hair was long, dark, and thick. It was so thick she often complained to Fonz about how sore her hands were after she had struggled to put all of her hair in one ponytail. Now her hair was so thin it could barely stay in the two French braids that draped over the sides of her face. Her skin color was darker than normal, and it seemed to barely be holding on to her small frame.

Fonz dropped his belongings and snatched the screen door open so hard and fast the screws on the hinges jerked, and the door opened as wide as it could. He wrapped his arms around his mother and held her as tight as her feeble body would allow. He closed his eyes tight and inhaled her lavender scent as a tear rolled down his face. Fonz knew that his mother had bad news to tell him. However, his heart was not ready to bear such a burden.

Mama Coolidge could feel her son's energy slowly draining out of his body. She had hoped that the cancer that was slowly eating away at her body would have gone away by the time her son was set free. It was her daily prayer that once they laid eyes on each other for the first time, she would have nothing but good news and blessed miracles to share with him. However, that was not the case.

"It's okay, baby. I'm sorry you didn't know. I told everyone not to tell you that your mama was sick. I just couldn't have that on your spirit while you were locked up in that horrible place. I just couldn't do it," Mama Coolidge explained to Fonz.

Fonz knew that he had to let go of his mother, but his arms just weren't getting the message that his brain was sending. He wished he had known so that he could have mentally prepared for what his eyes were about to see. But in reality, his mother was sick. The only person who always remained the same and whose love he could always depend on was possibly dying. There was no "good way" to receive that information.

Mama Coolidge was finally able to pull Fonz's arms apart. She instructed him to get his belongings off the porch and come inside. Dr. Williams had called ahead and told her the time that they should be arriving. She gathered up all of her strength and then some to make sure Fonz had a home-cooked meal waiting for him when he arrived.

Fonz went into his old room to put his stuff away. It looked nothing like it did when he'd called it home. His mom had taken down all of his football and gangster posters and painted the room a light toffee color. All of his old furniture was long gone and replaced with one queen-size bed, a dark wooden dresser, and a thirty-two-inch flat-screen TV. Plain horizontal blinds covered the windows.

"Baby! Come on out here and eat. I fixed all of your favorites," called out Mama Coolidge.

Fonz walked into the dining room to see more food on the table than he had seen in a very long time: smothered fried chicken, fried fish, meatballs in gravy, collard greens, candied yams, mac and cheese, mashed potatoes, dressing with cranberry sauce, a lemon-glazed pound cake, and a three-layer German chocolate cake. Fonz had no idea how he was going to eat all of this food, but he definitely was going to try.

As the mother and son sat down to eat, Mama Coolidge did the best she could to catch Fonz up on all that he missed. She told him about the small kitchen fire she had four years prior. She used the insurance money to update the entire house. She went on to tell him about the new neighbor across that street who had been cutting her grass for almost a year and refused to take any money and the ins and outs of the new supermarket that was built about four blocks away.

Fonz tried to be patient and let his mother volunteer the details of her sickness, but she clearly was beating around the bush. "Mama. What's wrong?" Fonz questioned.

"Nothing's wrong. Am I talking too much? I'm just happy to see you," she answered, still avoiding the topic.

Fonz shook his head and grabbed his mother's hand. "Mama. Stop it. You know what I'm asking. What's wrong with you? Your health? And where is Shawna? Didn't she know I was coming home?"

Mama Coolidge tried to smile, squeezing out a small smirk. She dropped her head, then placed her other hand on top of Fonz's.

"I have cancer, baby. Lung cancer."

Fonz cringed and fell from his chair, placing one knee on the carpet and his head in his mother's lap, covering the mournful sobs that floated from his deep voice. His tears were now a flowing stream. His worst nightmare was now a reality that he did not want to face.

Mama Coolidge continued to give the details of her illness. "I found out I had it two years ago. I had surgery to remove three tumors: one in my right lung, and two in my left lung. After that, I did chemotherapy for six weeks. They thought they got it all, and I was doing much better. A little less than six months ago, I felt a lump in my chest. I went to the doctor, and they said I had another tumor. This time they didn't want to operate, just a round of radiation. It's tough sometimes. Some days are better than others. I'm a survivor, baby. Mama is gonna fight."

Hearing the strength in his mother's voice was a wake-up call for Fonz. If she was not giving up, then there was no way he could. He lifted his head and used the inside of his shirt to wipe the tears that soaked his face. He kissed his mother on her forehead, then sat down at the table.

"How are you maintaining this house, Mama? It's too much for you to handle on your own. I will be working soon, so I won't be here every day all day to help," Fonz said.

"I don't know, Fonz. Sometimes a few ladies at the church come by and help me. I don't know where that sister of yours has been. She calls and checks on me. That she does do. But I haven't seen her in months. Maybe even a year," answered Mama Coolidge.

Fonz's mother sharing that she had not seen his sister in months raised some serious red flags for him. That was not like her at all, especially after he got locked up. He added that to the mental list he'd started in his head: *check on sister*.

"I have a few people I connected with who might be able to help me figure out how we can get you an in-home nurse, Mama. I'm going to do whatever I need to do to make that happen for you," promised Fonz.

His mother smiled with her eyes. She was happy her baby boy was home and that he was safe. That was good enough for her.

Their conversation was interrupted by a knock at the door. Mama Coolidge's face lit up, and her mood went from extremely sad to giddy, almost childlike.

"Go get the door," she instructed Fonz.

Fonz looked at his mother's face and knew that she was up to something. He walked over to the door, and what he saw caused his eyes to become filled with water. There on his mother's porch stood Elle and Li'l Fonz.

Elle had cornrow braids in her hair that shaped her face and brought out her eyes. She was wearing a long yellow dress with blue flowers that complemented her thick curves perfectly. She was a little heavier than she was the last time Fonz saw her, but she was still as beautiful as ever. Li'l Fonz had on a plain white T-shirt and a pair of colorful Air Max shoes. You could tell he had just gotten a haircut with a crisp lineup due to all of the little, fine hairs that covered the shoulders of his T-shirt. He had a diamond stud in his ear and a smile identical to his father's.

Fonz literally ran outside after opening the door and picked his son up in his arms. He hugged and kissed Li'l Fonz, causing him to giggle uncontrollably. Fonz's emotions were all over the place. To hold his son and see his Elle were things he had been dreaming of for many years.

"Man! I'm so happy to see you! You have gotten so big!" Fonz said to his son.

"I'm happy to see you too, Dad. We look alike," joked the handsome young man.

Fonz let out a roaring laugh. "We sure do! You look better though, man. I'll give you that."

Fonz looked over at Elle and started to get nervous. The feelings that he had when they were a couple all started pouring back in. Her personality and heart were just as beautiful as she was and let off an energy that was undeniable. Fonz wanted to grab and kiss her, but he knew that wasn't realistic. She had written him plenty of letters while he was away, and he knew what the deal was. She was in love with someone else. She was happy. Fonz had to respect that.

"Hey, old man. You looking good," said Elle as she stretched her arms out for a hug. Fonz fell right into her arms and embraced her like a man in love. Although his strong affection was a little uncomfortable for her, she allowed him to share that moment with her. Even though she had moved on with her life, she still cared about Fonz and wanted him to have a new start.

The three walked into the house to see Mama Coolidge. Elle gave her a hug followed by Li'l Fonz. "How you feeling, Granny? Did you make all of this food? I think you did too much. This is a lot," scolded Li'l Fonz. Everyone in the room laughed.

"Yes, I did. It was a special occasion, so I had to do something special," she explained.

That answer seemed to be good enough for Li'l Fonz. He gave his granny another hug and a kiss on the cheek, then proceeded to get a plate off the table and start filling it with food. Once he was done making his plate, Li'l Fonz went into the bedroom to watch TV. Big Fonz cut himself a piece of German chocolate cake and sat down at the table with Elle and his mother.

"I can't thank you enough for bringing him around so he could have a relationship with Mama while I was gone," Fonz said to Elle, looking her in the eyes and becoming hypnotized. "That meant more to me than you'll ever know. You're a great mother. My baby looks healthy and happy. A father can't ask for much more than that."

"You're welcome. But you don't have to thank me for that. I will always do what's best for him. Making sure he has a relationship with his dad's family is something that he needs. Now that you're home, he needs you, too," Elle shared.

Fonz became a little confused. "He needs me? What do you mean? Is something wrong?"

Elle shook her head. "No, silly. Nothing is wrong. I'm saying he needs you as his father. Yes, he has my fiancé to help provide for him and show him different things. At the end of the day, you are his father. You are what makes the world go 'round and 'round for him." Elle started to get choked up as her eyes became watery and a few tears fell onto her cheeks.

"Come on, E," pleaded Fonz. "Don't do that. Wipe them tears. I hear you. I'm going to get it together. Not just for Li'l Fonz but for his brothers and sister too. As for me, prison is not a place I want to ever be in again!"

"I hope so," replied Elle. "He's a good kid, but it's hard out here. So many influences to make him lose focus. He's approaching that age when he's going to need you more than ever."

Chapter Five

The programs at the reform center were not bad at all. Fonz signed up for some classes that fine-tuned the work that Dr. Williams had started. He was learning how to truly suppress the street side of him and be more polished and professional. The training was making him smoother in the game than he already was. The more he learned, the more he realized how much of a threat he was becoming, showing the professional side but still using his street smarts and savvy when he handled business. It was perfect.

Dr. Ose was a huge help. She worked with Fonz one-on-one often. Once she was privy to what his degree was in, she really took a liking to Fonz. She personally drafted his résumé for him. Dr. Ose helped him apply to several jobs. She would even take him to lunch with her sometimes.

Fonz thought she was extremely attractive but out of his league. She was stacked with perky breasts, a slim waist, a firm ass, and smooth dark-chocolate skin. She always wore high heels, which made her calves and butt pop out just right. Dr. Ose wore her hair in a bob that she kept cut and styled perfectly every day. He was most attracted to her lips. She had the sexiest lips. They were full but not big, with the dip in the middle of her top lip that she kept perfectly glossed. Fonz would catch himself daydreaming about outlining her lips with his tongue. He always snapped out of it quickly. He did not want to do anything to jeopardize his participation in the program.

Dr. Ose knew that Fonz was special early on during their interactions. He was charming and handsome, also motivated and inspiring. She would watch him offer assistance to the other program participants. He was always so patient with them. There was one participant named Craig who had a speaking impediment. It was hard for him to articulate what he wanted to say, and both he and the other participants would get frustrated and sometimes even argue with each other. Fonz started working with Craig every day, utilizing the things he learned from Dr. Williams and YouTube to help him with his speech. Shortly, Craig's speech was noticeably better, and he had more confidence in himself. Dr. Ose grew to become quite fond of Fonz and made his success in the program her personal responsibility.

One day when Fonz was walking out of the center on his way home, Dr. Ose called for him to come back to her office. As he walked in, right away he noticed that her assistant wasn't there, something that had never happened since he'd started attending the center.

"Hey, Doc. You wanted to see me?" Fonz asked curiously.

"Yes!" she responded eagerly. "I'm so glad I caught you. I think I have an opportunity that is perfect for you. You've been doing so well in the program I think you have earned the chance to go out in the world and use everything you've learned."

Fonz started smiling and could not control it. "Opportunity? A job? You have a job for me?"

Dr. Ose joined Fonz in his eagerness. "Yes! I have a job for you. A high-profile client of mine is in need of a chauffeur. He did not want to go through a hiring service. He's very private and did not want to take any chances. He asked me if I knew anyone who would be a good fit. I suggested you. The pay is great and will definitely cover your parole requirements. You will use his car to drive him around. The catch is there isn't a set schedule. You will have to be on call twenty-four seven. Whenever he calls, you have to make yourself available. Are you interested?"

"Hell yeah, I'm interested!" Fonz yelled out before he knew it. "I'm so sorry, Dr. Ose. That was an accident. I know that was not an app—"

In the middle of Fonz's apology, Dr. Ose pushed her lips against his and gently allowed her tongue to play with the tip of his tongue. Fonz was in total shock. It took him a few seconds to open his eyes after Dr. Ose pulled away. He could not believe what had just happened.

"Listen, Fonz, I like you . . . a lot. The more I'm around you, the harder it is becoming to hide my feelings. Don't get me wrong. Yes, I like you, but I'm not looking for a life partner or anything like that. Just a good friend who can help me unwind and relax from time to time," Dr. Ose explained.

Fonz was feeling Dr. Ose as well. He stood in front of her desk and listened to everything she said and saw straight through her. "Help you relax . . . is that code for fuck you good? You know, I'm still learning all of the new slang and terms," teased Fonz.

Dr. Ose was instantly turned on by Fonz's direct talk. She smiled and stood up from her chair. She slowly started to unzip her dress and let it fall off her nicely shaped body, allowing her matching black lace bra and panty set, trimmed in red, to be on full display.

"It definitely means that. Are you interested in this job as well?" she asked Fonz as she walked toward him. Once she was close enough, she reached out and grabbed his enlarged penis, which to her surprise was already nice and hard.

"Interested in fucking you good? That would be another hell yeah," Fonz answered sarcastically. "But I have to ask, if I say no, are you going to put me out of the program?"

Dr. Ose had started kissing Fonz on his neck. His question made her stop and step away from him. At that moment she realized how serious Fonz was about getting a fresh start on life, which intensified her attraction to him tenfold.

"Of course not!" Dr. Ose quickly answered. "I take my work here at the center very seriously. I would never do anything to jeopardize the integrity of the program and the men who come to us for help. You have my word that this offer is a hundred percent personal and has nothing to do with our business relationship. Even if the dick is trash, I'll still help you become a better you."

Fonz was relieved that Dr. Ose was not trying to use his participation in the program as a tool to hurt him. He did not want to repeat his mistakes of the past and the choices he made when it came to women.

Fonz pulled Dr. Ose to him and kissed her passionately. He took his right hand and pushed her panties to the side. His fingers were instantly drawn to her clit, and he began to massage it, causing her to let out moans through their kiss.

He pulled away and looked her in her eyes. "Ain't nothing trash about this dick, baby. Nothing!"

Fonz turned Dr. Ose around and pushed her down on her desk. The panties he pushed to the side now lay ripped on the floor. He pulled out his rock-hard penis and pushed it inside of her hard. She let out a small, pleasure-filled scream. Fonz did not want to cum quick, but it had been so long since he had been with a woman. Not to mention he had been sexually attracted to Dr. Ose since he first started the program.

Dr. Ose knew what Fonz was up to and was not having it. She looked over her shoulder back at Fonz and simply said, "Fuck me!" Like a well-trained puppy, Fonz started to slam his rock-hard dick in and out of her. She was so wet her juices were running down her legs. Fonz was hitting the spot that she had needed scratched for a very long time. Each in-and-out motion pushed her closer and closer to her climax.

Fonz tried with all of his power to not cum, but it was not working. Her pussy was so warm and wet, and it seemed to fit his dick perfectly. Dr. Ose's legs began to shake, and Fonz knew exactly what that meant. He sped up his pumps, causing Dr. Ose's moans to get louder and louder until they both yelled out at the same time, "I'm cumming!" Fonz's legs gave out on him, and he collapsed on top of Dr. Ose's back. He was a little embarrassed that he was only able to last such a short period, but at the same time he didn't care. They both were able to get one off, so as far as he was concerned, he did what he was supposed to do.

"That was exactly what I needed," Dr. Ose shared with Fonz. "I am going to need more of that."

Fonz's ego was boosted ten notches when Dr. Ose said she wanted more. "Absolutely, love. Your pussy is better than I imagined it would be. I will be more than happy to dick you down whenever you want it," Fonz responded proudly.

Dr. Ose smiled as she turned to face Fonz. "That's great to hear. Let's get ourselves together before housekeeping comes this way."

As the two were scrambling to get their clothes back on, Dr. Ose's phone rang. It was the high-profile client she had recommended Fonz to. She spoke to him briefly, then hung up the phone. "That was your new boss," she shared with Fonz. "He said he trusts me and my judgment, so you have the job. You start on Saturday. He's going to text you all of the information you need."

Fonz was on cloud nine. He got a great job and some great pussy all in the same day. His smile was big and bright. Life at that moment was amazing.

Chapter Six

Fonz's return felt incomplete. He had been home for almost four months and had seen or bumped into everyone but his sister, Shawna. The two of them were very close and always had been. Even though they were only two years apart in age, Fonz always felt obligated to be more of a father figure and protector than a brother. The older they became in age, that aspect of them always remained the same. Fonz knew something was wrong. Shawna was hiding something.

Mama Coolidge couldn't tell Fonz much about his sister. She knew that Shawna was dating a new guy who seemed to be treating her like a queen. He bought a brand-new, fully loaded black-on-black Jeep Cherokee for her birthday. They lived in a really nice loft not too far from downtown Detroit. Shawna had been a well-known and great hair stylist. She had been highly requested throughout the area. Since dating her new boyfriend, Shawana gradually stopped going to work, and her popularity was no longer buzzing around the city. Almost four years had passed, and very few people had seen her.

As convincing as his mother was, Fonz was not accepting that everything was just golden with the new couple. After calling his sister four times, she finally answered the phone.

Shawna said, "Hello."

"Damn!" said Fonz. "About time you answered the phone!"

"Hey, bro! What's up?"

"You tell me. I'm worried about you. I've been home for four months, and I have yet to lay eyes on you. What's going on?"

There was a long pause before Shawna responded to her brother. "I'm sorry, bro. I know I should have made an effort to see you by now. I've been really busy at the salon and trying to make sure all of our other businesses are in order. And you know Red was in that bad accident, so I've been busy taking care of him also."

"Wait. Did you say Red? As in the legendary Red off the block Red?"

"Oh, my God! Bro! Please do not tell anyone that Red is in the city, and please don't tell anyone that he's with me."

Shawna's voice was mixed with anxiety and fear. Stressed and afraid were not characteristics of Fonz's sister. He lay on his bed, staring at the ceiling and racking his brain, trying to figure out what to say to get her to open up.

"It's all good, sis. I won't say a word to anyone. Text me your address so I can come see you."

Shawna paced back and forth in the dimly lit living room. The only light that could be seen came from her cell phone and the glare from the TV. She was growing more and more nervous. She knew her brother just as well as she knew herself. She wasn't going to be able to stall him much longer.

"Fonz, let me call you right back."

"What? Call me back for what?"

"I have to do something really quick. Just give me five minutes."

"Five minutes, Shawna! That's it. You better call me right back."

"Okay. I promise. I'll call you back." She hung up.

Fonz's heartbeat began to speed up. Knowing that his sister was with Red did not sit well with him. Red was a hood legend. He was always deep in the robbery world. Red was a master in the game. No one was bigger or better than Red. He was a former football player who stood six feet five inches tall and easily weighed two hundred and sixty pounds, all solid muscle. The older Red became, the more he let his mustache and beard grow in, which made him look even more intimidating and mysterious. A lot of people from their neighborhood referred to him as Baby Suge Knight. He wore a low-cut fade, which enhanced the thick, dark eyebrows on his face. Those eyebrows were the feature that seemed to attract the ladies the most. Fonz had never heard anything grimy about Red with regard to how he treated women, but at the end of the day he was a street dude. Street dudes were infamous for being super possessive and controlling of their women.

As Shawna stood in the living room shifting through her thoughts, echoes of dogs barking rang out in the air. Shawna broke out of her trance and quickly ran over to the desk where all of the security camera monitors sat. As she scanned each monitor carefully, she noticed a cat running down the sidewalk. She found what exactly had triggered her dogs to make them bark like crazy.

Shawana's life had drastically changed in the last four years. She had a golden color that radiated off her like a ball of sunshine. She had long, naturally curly hair that she usually kept wrapped in a bun of some sort. She had a small upper body with a flat stomach and perky C-cup breasts. Her bottom half was stacked. Her ass-hip-thigh ratio was a man's dream. She was blessed with the booty many women don't mind breaking their banks in an attempt to duplicate. She never wore a ton of makeup and never had to. Shawna had ageless beauty, as if she were aging backward. However, since her boyfriend's accident, she had developed dark circles and bags around her eyes. Her skin didn't have its natural glow anymore. The change was very noticeable.

Shawna knew she could not hold off her brother any more than she already had. She slowly walked into the dark bedroom that sat in the back of the house, careful not to make too much noise.

"Baby?" she called out into the dark.

After a brief pause, a deep voice responded with a heavy, "What is it?"

"Do you remember me telling you about my brother, Fonz? The one who just got home from prison?"

"Yeah, I remember. I know Fonz and the crew he used to run with. What about him?" Red quizzed.

"It's been four months, and he really wants to see me. To be honest, I really want to see him too," answered Shawna, her voice trembling. "Not to mention I need to check on my mother."

At that moment a bright floodlight shone on Shawna. It shone so bright in her face that she had to lower her head into her shirt.

Red began to chastise Shawna. "What did I tell you about leaving this house? How many times have I talked to you about leaving this house without me? Why do you keep trying me, Shawna?" His voice boomed out like the beat on a bass drum.

"Baby, I'm not. I promise I'm not! I know what you said," Shawna replied quickly. Her words sounding muffled due to her head being partially covered by her shirt. "He's my brother. My only brother, Red. If he doesn't see me soon, he is going to start to worry. Please, baby. Please let me go see my family." Shawna was now on her knees, pleading, with tears running down her face. Each tear that hit the floor made Shawna weaker and weaker. She desperately wanted to hug her brother's neck and lay her head on her mother's shoulder. However, the vise grip that Red held on her did not appear to be loosening anytime soon.

Red did not mean to be so cruel and cold to Shawna. He loved her more than he loved himself. That love was often turned into fear, the fear of being left alone, the fear of Shawna finding someone else, someone better, someone who wasn't so fucked up in the head. Deep down inside, Red knew without a doubt that Shawna was the best thing that ever happened to him.

Shawna was working as the lead hair stylist in the salon where Red was getting his hair cut at the time. He noticed Shawna right away. She lit up the room. She had the aura of power surrounding her. Red had always been a low-key guy. Never said a whole lot, but made sure his presence was felt. Even though he noticed Shawna, he didn't say anything to her right away. She was always too busy, and he just didn't want the attention of striking up a conversation with her.

One day he walked into the salon, and to his surprise, Shawna did not have a client in her chair. He licked his lips, smoothed out his beard, and laid down his eyebrows as he walked toward her work station. As soon as he started walking in her direction, Shawna turned around, and the two of them locked eyes. When she turned her head around, her curly hair swung around as well, then bounced perfectly onto her shoulders.

Red was so handsome to Shawna. He was always well groomed and neatly cut. He had a naturally loud presence in a room without even trying or saying one word. He wasn't dressed flashy, nor did he have a ton of jewelry on. A simple black Polo shirt with a red horse-

man and the matching shorts was his outfit for the day. Retro 11 Jordan Concords were on his feet, and the scent of his Sauvage Dior cologne entered the room before he did, captivating Shawna and a few other ladies in the salon.

"Hey, Ms. Lady. How are you doing today?" Red asked, extending his hand to Shawna.

The tone in his voice gave her chills. When his hand touched hers, their souls seemed to connect instantly.

"I'm doing just fine now," Shawna replied, flirting like she had never flirted before. "How are you?"

Red gazed into Shawna's eyes, never breaking his stare. Everything about her was perfect in his eyes. Shawna had on some distressed jeans that showed off her hips and ass just right. Her black Puma cropped top lay perfectly on her body and matched her comfortable black-and-white Puma Classic Selects perfectly. Her thin silver hoops were semi lost in her curls, and her lips shone with a thin coat of clear lip gloss from Sephora. For a man like Red, who had many times in the past played upon the insecurities of women, a woman as confident and stunning as Shawna made Red step his game up to a level he wasn't used to playing on.

"Are you going to answer my question? Or just stare at me all day?" Shawna joked, seeing that she clearly had Red off his game. Shawna was playing tough, but the feeling was definitely mutual. She was a naturally confident woman, but there was something about Red that made her confidence intensify. She felt like her fly had to match his swag or he wouldn't be interested in her.

"My apologies. Wow, that's a first," admitted Red.

"A first? A first what?"

"The first time a woman has been so beautiful that she left me speechless," he replied as he slowly brought her hand to his mouth and softly placed a kiss on it.

A week later they went on their first date and became inseparable.

One thing that Shawna could definitely give Red credit for was helping her discover the full scope of her sexuality and her deep inner freak. Shawna had only been with three other guys before Red. They were selfish lovers. They would always get their nut and not do anything to make sure Shawna was satisfied. All of that changed when she met Red. The first time she knew he would be the man to change her life came from an interaction they shared during the first night they spent together.

The two were going to meet at Flood's for food and drinks. It started raining incredibly hard. Shawna did not like driving in the rain, so she called Red and canceled their date. He said he understood and he would call her later to reschedule. Thinking nothing else of it, Shawna got in the shower and put her PJs on. She wrapped her hair up in a pineapple-like style, allowing her curls to fall freely at the opening of her head scarf. Shawana was sitting on her couch, enjoying some butter pecan ice cream and watching TV, when there was a knock on her door. She wasn't expecting company and thought it must be one of her neighbors in her apartment building. She opened the door, and there stood Red, wet from head to toe, holding a plastic bag filled with all types of chips and candy.

"I thought you could use some company," Red said seductively.

"I like the way you think," Shawna replied. She opened her door wide, welcoming Red inside.

Shawna took the bag from Red and headed toward her kitchen. "The bathroom is the first door on the right. You can grab a towel from the linen closet right next to it," Shawn instructed Red. She started taking items out of the wet bag. "Ohhh, you got all the classic goodies. I think I have a pair of my brother's sweatpants on the back of my bedroom door if you want to take off those wet clothes," Shawna said as she continued to unpack the bag. She put the juice Red brought in the refrigerator. When she turned around, Red was standing behind her in nothing but a towel, still a little damp from the rain.

"Oh, my," a smitten Shawna blurted out.

Red smiled. He then grabbed her hand and led her into her living room and laid her down on the couch.

"What are you doing?" Shawna asked Red in a mist of confusion. Red never answered her. He just proceeded to pull down the boy-short panties she had on. He got on his knees and shifted her body so that her butt was on the edge of the couch cushion and her legs were on each side of Red.

Shawna didn't know why she was so comfortable with Red. Part of it was because of their connection, and part of her comfort was fueled by her curiosity. Before she could finish her thought, she felt Red's fat tongue licking her pussy. His tongue was so fat and wide, with one lick he covered her entire pussy. He licked and licked and licked, until her box was soaking wet with juices were running down her ass crack. He then took his magical tongue and started focusing on her clit. The way he cupped and hugged her sweet spot with his mouth was something she had never experienced before. She was moaning uncontrollably in ecstasy when Red then inserted his index and middle fingers deep inside of her. He pressed his fingers against the inside of her pussy in an upward motion and then vigorously started finger fucking her while sucking her clit.

At this point Shawna could barely breathe. Pleasure like this was not anything she had ever experienced before. It was incredible! She suddenly started feeling a sensation that was familiar. "I have to pee!" she yelled out in between a moan and a slight scream.

"No, you don't," answered Red. "Relax and let it go."

Shawna followed the orders given to her and just relaxed. She came so hard that she squirted all over Red's face. This excited Red more than it did her. He could tell that it was her first time ever doing that. Shawna lay there paralyzed. The only thing she could manage to get out was, "What did you do to me?"

Red grabbed her face and kissed her passionately. He then looked her in her eyes and said, "I gave you the pleasure that you deserve." He then took his large dick and inserted it into her extremely wet pussy. He put her legs on his shoulders and made love to her like it was all that ever mattered to him. Shawna was in pain in the beginning, unable to take a penis that big. After a few deep strokes, she got used to it and was able to enjoy every inch of it. After that night, Shawna was hooked. She got into porn and sex toys and was always open to try new sexual positions. She did everything she could to keep their sex life exciting and fresh.

Those days were a distant memory. Due to the accident, Red suffered from impotency. No matter what they did, he could not get an erection. They tried pills, yoga, stimulants, Ecstasy, and even another chick. Nothing worked. It had been four years since Shawna felt the girth of Red's twelve-inch penis inside of her. Not getting satisfied sexually just added another layer to the complicated and sad story of Shawna's life.

Red turned off the flood light he was shining in her face. He got off of the floor and walked toward her. The sound of Red's footsteps coming toward Shawna made her jump up off the floor like a ninja. When Red saw her jump, he knew that he had genuinely hurt her feelings.

Red grabbed Shawna with both arms and pulled her to his chest. He held her head with one hand and rubbed her back with the other.

"I'm sorry. I just can't have you out in the world without me. I would die if something ever happened to you," Red tried to explain.

Shawna had been here before and knew that she had to keep her answers short to avoid triggering the voices in Red's heads.

"I know," she managed to say in between her sniffles. "What if Fonz came here? What if he came and picked me up? Then you would know I'm not alone. I'll be with my brother, someone you know and somebody you know loves me just as much as you do." Shawna had never come up with an alternate plan before. She typically just shut down when Red went on his rage rants or started being mean for no reason.

Red was moved by her resiliency. He knew he had to attempt to meet her in the middle. "Just know that I'm not feeling this at all. But I love you, and I want your brother to know that you're safe. Call him back, and tell him he can pick you up and bring you back after you two go eat. Nothing more. You understand?" Red instructed Shawna.

"Yes. Yes, baby. I understand," Shawna replied as she grabbed Red's face with both hands and placed kisses all over it. "Thank you so much!" Shawna grabbed her phone off the floor and started to walk back into the living room to call Fonz.

"No! Make the call right here. I want to hear what you're saying. I just told you I don't like this shit!" Red barked.

Shawna didn't say one word back to Red. She turned around and walked back into the bedroom to call her brother.

"Hello," Fonz answered.

"Hey, bro."

"You okay?"

"Yeah! I'm good. I just had to take care of something."

"So when are you coming through?"

"I was thinking. How about you come here?"

"To your spot?"

"Yes. You can come pick me up, and we can go to the Hudson Café. That used to be our spot, remember?"

"Hell yeah. I haven't been there since I've been out either. I'm down."

"Perfect. What time are you free tomorrow?"

"I'll be by to get you at twelve thirty. Send me your address."

"Okay. I'll do it right now. I can't wait to see you."

"Same here, sis."

The two hung up. Shawna texted Fonz her address. For a second, Shawna almost forgot that Red was in the room with her until she looked up and saw him staring at her with a blank look. It was almost as if he were looking straight through her.

The next day, Shawna blended in concealer under her eyes. She had become a fairly decent makeup artist. She studied YouTube videos whenever she could to learn different techniques to get a natural look. Shawana had to find a way to mask the obvious changes in her appearance but not stir up too many questions because she was now wearing full-face makeup. She missed being in the salon and working with her clients. However, her new life did not allow room for that.

As she finished the final touches on her hair and makeup, she could see Red looking at her through the bathroom mirror. He had taken all of the doors off the hinges in each room and refused to put them back on. No matter where she was in the house, he needed to know what she was doing and be able to see her. She had zero privacy. Shawna hated it. She felt like she was in prison or being held hostage. What she hated even more was the mean monster Red turned into when he got upset.

"How do I look?" she asked Red in a flirtatious tone.

"You look good. Yep. You look damn good. I thought you said you were going to lunch with your brother," Red said.

Shawna raised her head and looked Red in his eyes. "I am. He's coming here first. Remember, baby?"

Red walked inside the bathroom with her. He placed his hands on her shoulders, then slowly traced her body with his hands. She was wearing a spaghetti-strap coral dress that fit her shape perfectly. It hugged her body up top, then gradually flowed freely away from her body all the way down to her ankles. The color complemented her skin tone impeccably. She looked amazing, which scared Red and started to heighten his paranoia.

As his hands began to travel back up Shawna's body, she could feel his grip getting tighter. His breathing was getting heavy as he pressed his mouth down on her ear. What she first thought were signs of affection were slowly turning into signs of intimidation.

"If you are going to eat with your brother, I don't understand why the fuck you have to look so damn good! You sure you're not going on a date? Your brother taking you to meet some other guy? Is that what's going on here? Huh, bitch? You're not slick. Your ass is not going anywhere. You're staying here!" Red now had his arm wrapped around Shawna's chest and was squeezing her tighter, staring at her through the mirror. He was screaming in her ear. Each word was getting louder and deafening.

Shawna started crying. The traces of her tears could be seen on her face like pathways of pain through her freshly applied makeup.

"No, Red. Why would you say that? Please relax, baby. I would never betray you like that. I love you. You are the only man for me," Shawna pleaded, trying to calm Red down. "I am going to lunch with my brother and only my brother. You can FaceTime me anytime while I'm gone to make sure. Please don't make me stay home. Please, baby." She slowly started to rub his arm while placing small, wet kisses on his bicep. Red's tight hold began to slowly loosen up.

Red literally started to shake his head, attempting to shake off the dark thoughts that were swarming in his head. He knew how much this outing with Fonz meant to Shawna, and he wanted to make her happy. However, the other side of him was slowly started to creep its way in.

"I know. I'm sorry," Red whispered, lowering his arm and removing the hold he had on her. "Clean your face off. You need to look nice for your brother."

As Shawna watched Red walk away, her heart grew heavy for her love. She knew deep down inside he was still the same loving and compassionate man she fell in love with. The demons that had appeared and claimed residency in his head came after his accident, constantly suppressing the real Red. She had to figure out a way to get him back to his old self, starting with making him take his medication every day.

Getting him to take it at all was a struggle in the beginning, but as time went on, she was able to talk him into taking it more often. One of the side effects of the medication was severe drowsiness. Red's paranoia led him to believe that that was why Shawna wanted him to take the pills, to make him fall asleep so she could leave him or have someone hurt him. The battle was a hard one to fight, but Shawna refused to give up on him.

In fact, his medicine making him fall asleep almost *did* allow Shawna to finally get some dick in her life when Red was in the process of installing the high-tech security system that they currently had. He had ordered all of the parts and materials online. After a while, Shawna started to become familiar with the FedEx deliveryman. His name was Devin, and he was a cutie pie. He had fair skin and green eyes, an athletic build, and he wasn't too big or too small. The part of him that caught Shawna's attention was the tattoo artwork he had on both of his arms. Shawna had a thing for tattoos, especially sleeves.

One day, Red had taken his medication and was in the bedroom sound asleep. Shawna was cleaning up a mess he had made earlier installing some cameras when she heard a horn beep twice. That was the signal she and Devin had decided on to let her know she needed to put the dogs up. She put the broom down, locked the dogs in their room, and opened the door for Devin so she could sign for Red's packages.

When she opened the door, Devin was taken aback by how sexy she looked. Shawna had on a PINK blue and white tank top with matching leggings. Her curls were hanging wildly with a few of them falling in her face. As she signed for the packages, she could feel Devin staring at her.

"Go ahead and say it," she encouraged him.

Shocked by what he had just heard, Devin asked, "What do you mean?"

"I see you looking at me, so go ahead and say what's on your mind." Shawna had a feeling she knew what it was, but she wanted to hear him say it.

Devin shook his head no. "I can't do that. I want to be respectful."

His response confirmed Shawna's suspicions. Her pussy started throbbing at the thought of possibly being able to enjoy some dick. She turned around and started walking back into her living room, taking his signature pad with him.

"Um, excuse me, Ms. Shawna. I need that back," he said, pointing to his equipment.

"I know. Come and get it," she challenged him as she set the pad down and started to pull her shirt over her head.

Devin was only 24 and full of cum. She only had to ask him once. He stepped in, closing the door behind him. When he reached Shawna, she wasted no time. She reached down and grabbed Devin's dick. It was already nice and hard. It wasn't as thick as Red's, but it would do for now. Devin wasted no time either. He started to kiss Shawna on her neck, making his way down to her chest. He pulled her bra straps off her shoulders, making it easy to pull out one of her breasts. He massaged her nipple before he put her breast in his mouth. He flicked her nipple with his tongue and then began to bite on it softly. His other hand was squeezing Shawna's butt and was starting to make its way to her pussy when she made him stop. Guilt had crept into her heart and thoughts.

"Okay, stop. Please just stop," she directed Devin. "I can't do this."

"Come on, Ms. Shawna. Don't do me like this. You feel how hard my dick is? Do you know how long I've been wanting you?" he pleaded with her. "Just let me taste it."

Shawna pushed Devin back with a little force this time. "I said no!"

Devin just stood there with a look of utter confusion on his face.

"I'm sorry. But I know that Red would be absolutely destroyed if he walked out of that bedroom and saw us. More importantly, I know he would kill us both."

Devin's eyes became wide and were popping out of his face. "He's here? You're crazy!" he yelled at Shawna as he scurried to tuck in his shirt, grabbed his signature pad, and damn near ran out of their home.

Shawna locked the door and flopped down on the couch. She had mixed emotions. She was mad at herself for letting go of some young dick that she desperately needed to get. She was also disappointed in herself for almost violating her commitment to Red. One thing she was not confused about was that she was extremely horny. She had started something that she now was going to have to finish.

There was a video in her phone that she kept. It was video of her and Red having one of their many phenomenal sex sessions. She whipped out her cell phone, found the video, and hit the play button. Just looking at Red's erect penis made her pussy wet. Before the accident, he was without a doubt the best she had ever had.

Shawna pulled down her leggings and panties, spread her legs open, licked the tips of her fingers, and started rubbing her clit. As she watched the video, she took herself back to the times when every stroke of Red's penis hit a spot inside of her that made her yell out in pleasure. He turned her into a squirter and changed the way she experienced orgasms. Before she knew it, she had rubbed her clit so much that her body started to explode, creating multiple wet spots on her couch. Once she caught her breath, she got the fabric cleaner and cleaned up her mess before Red woke up.

Chapter Seven

Fonz pulled up to the address Shawna had sent. It was nothing like he expected. It was not a nice loft like his mother had said. It was a plain gray home with a gate wrapped around the entire property and a connecting gate that started in the middle of the driveway. He could see what looked like the top of a black SUV on the other side of the gate. He assumed it was the birthday present Red had given to Shawna.

Fonz parked on the curb, grabbed the bouquet of colorful flowers he'd bought for his sister out of the passenger seat, opened his door, and headed toward the house. The closer he got to the driveway, an overwhelming stench of dog shit flooded the air, followed by the vicious barking of what sounded like dangerous dogs. Fonz stop dead in his tracks.

When Shawna heard the dogs barking, a gigantic smile came across her face. She knew that meant her brother was outside. When she walked into the living room, Red was already there looking at the security monitors.

"Is that him?" Red questioned.

Shawna was so excited she could barely get her words out. "Yes, that's him. Go get your kids, babe."

"The kids" was the code name Red and Shawna used when referring to the dogs. Ten red-nose vicious pit bulls surrounded their home twenty-four seven. It was one of the security measures that Red insisted on having. The downside to having all of these pets was the extensive care and upkeep that came with owning them.

Red went over to a side door of the house that was partially blocked by a dresser. He opened the door and stepped out into their yard that couldn't be seen from the street. Red clapped his hands three times, then yelled loudly, "*Ven aqui, mis hijos!*" which means "Come here, my sons" in Spanish. All ten dogs came running as fast as they could. Once they reached the side of the house where Red was standing, he then yelled, "Be still!" All the dogs sat down, not moving an inch. He pushed a black button that was on the wall to the left of the door, and a gate slid from the house on the outside, closing the dogs in. Red closed the door to the house and slid the dresser back over. He walked into the living room and gave Shawna the nod of approval. She pushed a couple of buttons on the keyboard next to the monitors, and the gate in the driveway opened up.

Fonz was startled by the gate opening, unsure if the dogs would come running out. Once he saw that it was safe, he proceeded to walk up the driveway. The SUV looked as though it had not been driven in months. A heavy layer of dust had formed all over it. The grass in the yard was a mixture of green with brown patches and needed to be cut. The stench of the dog waste was so strong it was making Fonz gag. Something was not right. He had not made it inside yet, and he was already bothered and highly concerned. His sister would never under any circumstances live like this.

He continued to walk when he saw an arm directing him to come their way. When he got to the door and stepped inside, he almost broke down. The house was dim and gloomy. Only a sectional and a TV were in the living room. The windows were covered by drawn shades, allowing only a small amount of sunlight to invade the room. To the left was a small table with seven small TV monitors stacked on top of each other. Fonz was able to see on one monitor that the dogs were still on the premises. The room was muggy and smelled like a damp basement due to there being no sunlight or fresh air circulating through the home. There were ten different types of deadbolt locks on both of the doors he could see. Fonz was so distracted by what he was seeing, he looked right past his sister.

"Are those for me?" Shawna asked sarcastically.

Fonz blinked back to reality and finally saw the brown beauty who was his sister standing in front of him. "Oh, shit. Yeah, bighead. They're for you!" Fonz replied before laughing and hugging his sister, picking her up and spinning her around. Shawna hugged him just as tight, wrapping her arms around his neck and squeezing as hard as she could.

"Wow, look at you, girl. You look good. Just as ugly as you wanna be," Fonz teased Shawna.

She couldn't help but laugh. That was how they paid compliments to each other. They said the opposite of what they really meant. By Fonz calling her ugly, she knew he was really saying he thought she was really pretty.

"And I see prison reformed everything but your face," said Shawna, returning the favor.

"Ha! Good one!" laughed Fonz.

As they were talking, Fonz could feel a presence in the room, but he couldn't see anything or anyone. The room was dark considering it was twelve thirty in the afternoon, and it was hard for his eyes to adjust. Just as he was about to abandon the challenge of seeing if there was someone else in the room, he saw a figure that almost made him take off running.

Red walked slowly from behind the wall that separated the living room from the hallway. His body was nothing more than a shadowy figure until his face moved into the slither of sunlight in the room. Fonz was speechless. He was not expecting to see the person who'd walked in the room. The face that was always well groomed and caught the attention of all the ladies was now a scarred and matted mess. Two gruesome scars were displayed. One went from the top right corner of Red's forehead and stretched across his face to the other side of his nose. The other scar started just under his left eye and ended under the left side of his chin. They were the only things Fonz could focus on. In addition to that, over half of Red's right eyebrow was replaced by what appeared to be a keloid from a wound that had not healed properly. His beard was spotty and looked like it was stuck to his face with Krazy Glue.

"What's up, Fonz? Welcome home," Red greeted Fonz, trying to break the ice.

"Thanks, man," Fonz managed to squeeze out. "I'm sorry. You good, Red? What happened to you?"

"Really, Fonz?" Shawna asked, hitting Fonz in the shoulder, embarrassed by her brother's question.

"It's cool, baby. We knew he would be shocked when he saw my face," Red said, trying to calm Shawna down. "A while ago, I was in a really bad car accident. My head went through the windshield, which is how I got all of these scars on my face."

"My bad, man. I didn't know," Fonz apologized. "Grateful you're still here with us." He extended his hand to give Red a handshake and a hug. Red was a little hesitant but eventually accepted Fonz's gesture and reached his hand out in return.

Shawna was becoming emotional, so she decided to break up this sentimental reunion. "Come on, bro. You know it starts to get crowded around this time. I want to be able to get a good seat."

"Right, right," agreed Fonz. He turned and looked at Red again. "It was good seeing you, OG."

Red nodded his head at Fonz. "Same to you. Glad you're back in the world with us."

On the way to the café, Fonz and Shawna talked about their childhood memories and fun times they had when their mom was at work and they were home alone. Fonz knew his sister was not in a good place, but that wasn't what he wanted to focus on right away. It was their first time seeing each other in more than six years. He was able to find an open parking space on the street not too far from the restaurant. As he was parking, he thought there was one thing they should talk about before they went inside.

"Hey, sis. You know Mama's not doing well, right?" Fonz asked in a concerned tone.

Shawna dropped her head. "I had a feeling. What's wrong?"

"The cancer is back. She's getting radiation treatment, but the doctors aren't sure it's going to work this time." Fonz turned and looked out the window, trying to keep his composure.

Shawna began to sob. "I should have been there for her. I can't believe I let her go through that alone. Oh, Mama."

Fonz reached over and consoled his sister. Her tears were painful for him to see. He did not want her to be sad. But he knew nothing he could say would take away the guilt she was feeling.

"Hey. Come on now. You know Mama is a fighter. She's in great spirits. She's not giving up, and we can't either. We have to stay encouraged and positive. You feel me, sis?" It wasn't the most poetic, but it was all Fonz had.

Shawna went into her purse and pulled out some tissue. She started to dab the tears on her face, hoping not to smudge her makeup too much. "You're right. It just breaks my heart. Mama is such a wonderful woman. I hate to think about her suffering or being in pain."

Fonz agreed. "Yes. You are dead on, sis. But listen, I'm hungry, so let's get in here and eat."

Shawna held her brother by the arm as the two walked into the restaurant. They sat down and enjoyed the great food. Fonz filled Shawna in on his new job and his great success at the center, and they continued to reminisce about the good times they'd shared together in the past.

On the way back to drop Shawna off, Fonz could no longer hold his tongue. He had to find out what was going on with his baby sister. "All bullshit aside, Shawna, what the fuck is going on?" he asked.

Shawna closed her eyes and took a deep breath. She knew this talk was coming. "What?" she responded, trying to act surprised by his question. "What are you talking about?"

Fonz was starting to grow irritated with her facade. "Shawna! Stop with the bullshit! Is that nigga beating on you? Don't think I didn't notice all that damn makeup on your face. What the fuck are you hiding?"

"No! I promise he has never hit me," she said passionately, trying to convince Fonz that she was okay. "I wouldn't lie about that, bro. I would tell you."

"What is up with him? The man I saw today is not the same Red from back in the day. That shit hurt my heart. I wanted to talk some business with him, but I don't know anymore. That's probably not a good idea at all."

Shawna was a smart woman and able to read between her brother's lines. "Business? You got a job you working on, bro?"

Fonz shook his head. Him and his big mouth. He had never lied to his sister, and he wasn't about to start now. "Maybe. I don't know yet. You remember my new job I was telling you about?" Shawna nodded her head yes.

"The guy I drive for is some sort of high-end painter. A real square. A rich square. Sometimes when I'm working, he has me take him to pick up large amounts of money from his attorney. When it's the weekend, the cash is with him at his house until he flies out again or goes to the bank on Monday. I'm thinking about getting that nigga."

Shawna hung on to everything Fonz was saying, word for word. "You gotta let Red in on this, bro. You have to!"

"I don't know, sis. That's not the same Red," said Fonz.

"You're right. The accident changed him. A lot. He suffers from schizophrenia and is ridiculously paranoid. I'm pretty sure you figured that out by now."

Fonz let out a small chuckle. "Yeah. The surveillance system, man-eating dogs, and ten deadbolt locks on the door, not to mention the remote-control gate, all let that secret out of the bag." Fonz quickly stopped laughing when he realized Shawna did not see the humor in any of it. "My bad," he apologized.

"You have no idea what I go through. He's so afraid that something is going to happen to me that he's afraid to let me go anywhere by myself. He has texted me fifteen times since I've been with you. He does get a little scary sometimes, I can admit that."

Shawna saw how those words changed the expression on Fonz's face, and she needed to clean that up quickly.

"He doesn't get abusive, just scary. When he takes his medicine, he's fine and it's not as bad. That's when he has moments where the old Red surfaces, so I know he's in there. He just needs something to help bring him back permanently. To remind him of the legend and great man he is. He needs this job, Fonz. Please. Do this for me. Help me get my life back."

Fonz's heart hurt for his sister. For Red too. Red was the man. To see him in the condition he was in now was soul crushing. Knowing that it was also hurting his sister almost forced him to let Red in.

"I'm not saying yes, but I'm not saying no. Let me think about it," Fonz finally answered Shawna.

Shawna smiled and grabbed her brother around the neck and hugged him with all of her strength. She had a feeling he was going to give her what she'd asked for.

Chapter Eight

It had been a few hours, and the three of them just sat in the living room in awkwardness. Shawna, Red, and Bless sat there, all of them tending to their personal thoughts. The only sound was the subtle hum of the house's ventilation system. Shawna grew tired and bored of the tension and walked over to the television and turned it on. Bless's eyes followed her as she walked across the room, and Red's eyes were locked on him.

The *Martin* show was on the television screen, and it broke up the monotony that was present in the room. Shawna went to sit down next to Red, and everyone focused on the big screen. A classic scene played: one of the characters wrestled a stuffed dog. Instantly, Bless and Shawna giggled simultaneously. Red watched without any emotion. It seemed as if his sense of humor had been lost as of late. Although Bless was in a compromised position, the scene was much too funny, and he had to laugh. Nevertheless, Red didn't find the show funny. He also didn't find it funny that his woman was sharing a laugh with another man.

Red instantly grew enraged when he looked at Shawna, who seemed to be laughing a little too much for his liking. He raised his gun and aimed it at the television screen. Red fired five shots into the screen, causing the glass to shatter, and small sparks began to fly out of the electronic appliance. Shawna screamed and placed her hands over her ears to use as earmuffs as the shots rang out. As the mounted television hung there demolished with multiple bullet holes, everyone's eyes were on it.

Breathing heavily, Red stared at the screen with a demonic scowl. He then looked at Shawna and clenched his jaws tightly, displaying his disapproval at her comfort. Shawna dropped her head, not wanting to challenge him by staring too long. She knew better than to make him feel any negative emotion while he was having a rage episode. Shawna stood up and walked across the room with her head still down looking at the floor. Red watched as she walked away and then focused his attention on Bless, who was looking confused and worried.

Red stood up and slowly walked over to Bless. Red stared at him with hatred with every stride, not breaking eye contact with him. Without warning, he struck Bless in the jaw, causing his glasses to fly off and slide across the floor. Red looked down and smiled at Bless as he panted and smiled. Bless moaned as he felt the agony of Red's assault. Red struck him again, making his lip instantly split open, gushing blood.

Red had gotten out his aggression, and it was a release for him. He felt good seeing that someone was suffering. Shawna had seen enough and slowly walked up to Red. She rubbed his back, knowing that if she didn't stop him, Red could possibly kill Bless.

"Okay, baby, that's enough," she said with hesitation and care, not wanting to trigger him any further. "If you kill him, we can't get the money."

Red's shoulders dropped, and it seemed as if his tension and rage were subsiding. He knew that Shawna was telling the truth. They needed Bless alive so he could get the money from Watson. She slowly pulled Red away from Bless, directing him toward the kitchen. Facing Red, Shawna slowly rubbed his chest in an attempt to calm him. She felt his heart pounding, like a raging baboon was inside of it. Red's heart beat fiercely while his chest heaved up and down. He felt like a raging bull, but Shawna's slow chest rubs and soothing voice calmed his anger.

Shawna whispered softly to Red, then placed her head on his chest until he had calmed completely down. "Maybe you should take your medication to take the edge off," she suggested as her heart pounded as well. Shawna knew Red too well and could tell if a manic, schizophrenic episode was near.

It was always a progressive blowup with Red, and Shawna always felt the shit end of the stick. She had no choice but to recommend that Red medicate himself. There was too much on the line for him to mess it up.

Red thought about his actions toward Shawna earlier and felt remorse. So he nodded his head in agreement. Shawna sighed in relief. She quickly walked over to her bag and pulled out his prescription bottle.

"But this shit is going to knock me out cold. You know what that Lithium shit does to me," he said.

"I know, but what happens if you don't take it?" Shawna asked, giving him the cold and honest truth about the alternative outcome. She could see Red contemplating her words and his actions. Without hesitation, Shawna opened up the bottle and dropped two pills into her palm. "Just take these, and I can hold it down while you rest. We have to be here all night, so we have to go to sleep anyway. We can sleep in shifts. What's the most he can do? He's tied up," Shawna recommended. "Here take it," she said as she lifted the pills to his mouth.

Red hesitantly opened his mouth, and she dropped the two pills on his tongue. He then threw his head back and swallowed them. "Okay, baby. I'm about to lie down and calm myself. I can feel myself slipping," Red admitted.

"Don't worry. I got you. I got us," Shawna said as she reached down and slowly grabbed the gun away from him. She watched as Red walked into the backroom, then turned her focus on Bless. She walked over to his glasses that were on the floor and picked them up. She placed them on his face, feeling sorry for Bless.

"Thank you," he whispered as he squinted, trying to maneuver his glasses onto the bridge of his nose.

"Don't thank me. I just felt sorry for your goofy ass," Shawna said rudely, not wanting to show him any slight weakness or glitches in her loyalty armor.

Chapter Nine

It was approaching the twilight hour of the morning. Bless closely watched as the woman tried to fight her sleep. She periodically nodded off and jerked up, catching herself before her chin could touch her chest. At that point, sleep was getting the best of her, and Bless's mind began to churn. He was trying to figure a way out of the sticky predicament he was in. Bless tried to wriggle his hands from the rope ties, but it was to no avail. It was too tight and secure. His sweaty palms began to shake, and he faintly began to feel numbness in his fingertips from the restricted circulation. His wrists were raw from hours of being tied up, and his ass ached from the wooden chair.

Bless studied her closely, looking for an entryway to have a conversation. It had been a couple of hours since Red had fallen asleep in the bedroom, and Bless knew that he was running out of time. Shawna, still with the gun in her hand, looked at Bless. She saw him staring at her, which made her grow alert. She quickly stood up and shook her head, trying to shake off the fatigue.

"You got coffee?" she asked nonchalantly as she looked toward the kitchen.

"Yeah, it's right next to the fridge. The coffee is in the cabinet, directly above it," he answered.

"Cool," she said as she headed in the direction of the kitchen.

As she walked away, Bless caught a glance of her plump buttocks and slim waist. Her frame was unique.

He'd never seen a slim woman with hips as wide as hers. Although she wore a long, flowing skirt, her hips were still visible. He could tell she was a gym fanatic. For the first time in a long while, he felt aroused by a woman. Bless didn't have much time to think about anything else since the passing of Queen. He began to watch closely as her weight shifted from one side to the other as she swayed her hips back and forth on her way to the kitchen.

Her sundress didn't hide her curves, and her assets effortlessly shone through the fabric. Bless watched as the woman stood on her tiptoes to reach the coffee. Her small feet were manicured and flawless as she stretched out her body, flexing her calf muscles. Bless looked over at the couch she had been sitting on, noticing she left the gun sitting on the cushion. He instantly realized that she was sloppy or too sleepy to stay on point. He began to ponder ideas that could help him out of the current jam.

About ten minutes later, after the coffee was done, Shawna returned to the living room. "Why do you let him talk to you like that?" Bless asked as she blew in her coffee mug, trying to cool down the steaming brew.

"Excuse me?" Shawna said as she snapped her head up and shot a menacing glare at Bless.

"No disrespect. But I'm just wondering why a woman of your caliber and beauty lets someone talk to her like that," Bless said.

"Shut the fuck up! You don't know what the fuck you're talking about," she said, instantly growing defensive.

Shawna set down her coffee and picked up the gun. She stormed over to Bless and hit him with the butt of the gun, cracking his glasses. She clocked him right on his temple, making him release an agonized grunt. Blood began to trickle from the gash on the side of his head. She stood over Bless, panting heavily as pain and anger boiled. Her heart was racing, and she couldn't contain the rage that brewed inside of her. Bless had hit a nerve with his words, and she couldn't control her emotions. She had to release her hurt, and it came at the expense of Bless. They both were silent and remained quiet until the tension subsided.

"I didn't mean to upset you. I just noticed the tone he uses with you and the blatant disrespect. It's not right," Bless pleaded.

She placed the cold steel of the gun against his temple. Bless instantly began to plead with her.

"Listen. Listen. Just hear me out," he said as his eyes began to blink rapidly. Bless was extremely nervous. He tried to look past the barrel and into her eyes as she stood over him. He continued in a low, pleading tone, "I did not mean to offend you. I just noticed the way he looks at you. The way he treats you isn't a language of love."

"You don't know shit about my nigga. You don't even know the half of it, so I advise you to close your mouth and relax before he wakes up. I'm pretty sure you wouldn't be saying this to his face," Shawna said in defense of her man.

"You're right. I apologize," Bless conceded.

Shawna pulled the gun from Bless's head and stared at him with hatred. Deep inside, she knew that it was the truth of the matter, and what Red used to be like invaded her thoughts. She took a deep breath and slowly walked back to the couch and flopped down on it. She did not want to admit it, but Bless's words hit home because they were the truth. Red wasn't the same person she had fallen in love with years back. She wanted to explode in anger because Bless's word felt like daggers through her heart.

"You're not qualified to speak about a nigga of his stature. You are a sucker! That's why you're tied to that chair. You know what they say about suckers: at some point they're going to get licked. You four-eyed bastard!" she said, mocking him as she gritted her teeth in anger. Shawna couldn't believe a guy who was obviously not street even commented on a man like hers.

Bless watched her and studied her discomfort. He knew that his words had struck a chord. Bless saw that he had angered her, and he didn't want to push her any further than he already had. "I'm sorry," he whispered as he dropped his head.

Shawna grew uncomfortable and her blood boiled. She wanted to wake Red up, but she knew from past experience that waking him up while he was on his medication was a recipe for disaster. Shawna caught herself breathing heavily and staring a hole through Bless's head in rage as she gripped the pistol tightly in her hands, clenching her jaws and making her muscles bulge.

Bless looked up at her and saw the look of a crazy woman, and he thought that any moment steam would be coming out of her nose. Bless knew that he had evoked emotion from her, and that had been his main goal. He slyly tried to work his way back in.

"So what kind of man was he? I know at some point he was different," Bless nervously said.

"You have no fucking idea. That man back there is a king. Before the accident, you could have never filled his shoes," she said with aggression as her heart fluttered. Tears began to well up in her eyes. The hope that the old Red would return was the only reason she was sticking around.

Shawna woke up every day hoping he would return to the same man he used to be. She fought to bring the old Red back, but she'd started losing herself in the process. Like some other women, she'd fallen in love with the idea of a man rather than actually getting to know the man standing in front of her. Shawna missed the old Red, the

Red who treated her like gold. She closed her eyes, and her thoughts began to jog backward to a time when love was blissful and blind in her world.

With a fresh, unscathed face, Red stared into space as he lay on the fluffy white pillows. The sunbeams peeked through the blinds and hit him perfectly, giving him the warmth of the morning sun. His freckles seemed to be flawlessly splattered on his face as if God personally crafted the perfect imperfection. He looked down at the woman who was in his arms sleeping peacefully. Red smiled at the curvaceous woman, admiring her naked body and thick frame. He smiled at her as he leaned down to kiss her on the forehead. As his lips touched her skin, she slowly moved and smiled before opening her eyes. She giggled lightly when she felt his hand palm her right butt check.

"Good morning, my love," Red whispered just before following up with more kisses. He turned his body so he could hover over her. She lay on her back and looked up at her man. The chain on his neck dangled down and swayed back and forth in front of her face like a hypnotizing pocket watch.

Red slowly slid his body down and was face-to-face with her center. He slowly began to kiss her love below, French kissing her lower lips as if they were the ones above. He was taking his time and being gentle. He took his two index fingers and slowly parted her lips. Her growing love button began to protrude from the pink ocean. Red slowly began to please his woman. She squirmed and grasped at the bedsheets, trying to get away from him. Red grabbed her by her thighs, pulling her back down to his flicking tongue. He paused in the middle of the blissful chaos and looked up at her, catching her eyes.

"I love you, Shawna," he whispered with his goatee covered in her sweet essence.

"I love you too, Red," she answered in a low, orgasmic voice. Red dove back in, working his tongue just the way Shawna had instructed him to.

A while later, Red was lying in bed, watching as Shawna stood in the steamy, hot shower. The sounds of the running water relaxed him as he slowly toked on a skinny weed-filled cigar. He watched closely as Shawna's ass cheeks touched the glass, fogging it up as her ass spread against it. He smiled as he blew smoke circles into the air. Red looked around the luxury condominium and felt accomplished. His career as a hired gun had finally gotten him to a position of comfort. Red had been through a lot in his 25 years on earth. From juvenile detention centers and boys' homes, he eventually graduated to prison once he became a legal adult. Red's skin tone was bright yellow, but his insides were dark.

Red's soul was tormented. People like him never had a chance to succeed. He never truly was shown love, so giving love was hard for him. It wasn't that he didn't want to love someone. He just didn't know how to do it properly. He was always alone mentally even if he was in a roomful of people. Red, naturally, was an outcast because he didn't look like anyone around him. He was too rough for the pretty boys, and he was judged and underestimated by the hard knocks. He honestly just never fit in. Red never could find his way because he didn't have anyone to guide him. The cold world created and molded Red to be a cold-blooded killer. However, that all changed when he met Shawna. Shortly after meeting her, he began to discover who and what he was.

Discovering Red's true talent didn't come without a high cost. He did a few prison stints because of his ignorance. Every time he had encounters with the law, it was because someone snitched on him or moved sloppily, which always led authorities back to him. Murder for hire was how Red found his true calling. He liked the fact that that line of work only required one or two people, which lowered the risk of getting caught. Red established a great reputation in the underground circuit among the drug dealers in the state. Word of mouth was his biggest advertisement, and he was considered the best in the game. If you wanted it done right and without it getting traced back to you, you hired Red. Plain and simple.

At some point, Red stopped keeping count of the murders. The myth in the streets was that he had more bodies than he had freckles. Statements like that gave Red an adrenaline rush, and he embraced his legendary boogeyman status. He wore it like a badge of honor. It was as if his job came from the depths his soul. That was the only explanation and reasoning behind the bold and heartless Red.

Red was at the end of his stint as a shooter and was ready to hang up his twin Glock pistols. He had a big job lined up that paid more than he had ever made. Word had gotten back to him that there was an open bounty on a Flint hustler for half a million dollars. Until that point, all of Red's hit jobs were under $10,000. It was a mission of every shooter's dream. Old timers who knew about the murder game called it an "exit wound." It was the one job that relocated your family and allowed you to retire. The thought of it made him smile at the possibilities. He stood up and entered the bathroom where Shawna was showering. As he continued to smoke, he spoke to his leading lady.

"Tomorrow is the big day," Red said as he puffed away.

"I know. I can't wait to leave this city and start our new lives," Shawna said, imagining their new start

minus the bullshit. Red had been promising her for months that, after this hit, they would leave town and start their new path down South. Shawna wasn't new to the street life because her brother had been in the streets all his life. However, the constant murdering was what she couldn't handle. Many nights Red would come in with the stench of blood on his clothes and the smell of gunpowder on his hands. She was tired of burning his clothing after jobs and worrying if karma would come knocking at his door in the middle of the night. Red promised her that this upcoming hit would be his last, and he would just sit back and sell weed down South, a much safer option.

"That's right, baby. We are out of this hellhole after I finish this up for the Irishman. This is going to set us up for life. I'm tired of being the boogeyman. I want to sit back, relax, and watch this money flow in," Red said as he smirked and took a deep pull of the weed.

Red put out his joint and set the half-smoked joint on the sink. He then slid off his boxers and stepped into the shower. Shawna wiped the water from her face and looked at her naked man hovering over her. She then looked down at his blessing and smiled. She instantly reached down and began wake up his manhood.

"There you go, baby," he cooed as he smiled, leaning down to kiss her forehead. He loved Shawna because she was a sexual being. She wanted it multiple times a day, and he had no problem obliging her requests. Red was sure she was a nymphomaniac. Just the sight of her naked body aroused him. She took him into her mouth as the water crashed against his stomach.

"One more week, we will be doing this on a beach somewhere. I promise," he said as he fell back against the wall and closed his eyes.

Chapter Ten

Red staggered into the master bedroom of Bless's home. The California-king bed was a far cry from his usual resting place back home. He fell onto the humungous bed, and it felt like a cloud of pillows. Everything was bright white and clean, and the scent of lavender gave it a heavenly vibe that instantly relaxed him. Red turned on his back as he looked around the room. He saw a red fox statue on the dresser and smiled at the porcelain piece. For some reason, it made him laugh out loud. Maybe it was the drugs kicking in. For whatever reason, it tickled him. He then looked just above it and saw a few monitors on the wall that showed every single room in the house and also the outside of the house. Red felt his eyes getting heavy, and the effects of the medication began to take him to his only place of solace: his dreams.

Red honestly wanted to treat Shawna well because he did love her. However, after the accident, things were never the same. He found himself not being able to control his emotions in any facet. It was almost as if Red was outside of his body at times and acted as a bystander during manic episodes. The wave of guilt would come almost every time when he took his pills and the harsh reality set in of how he had treated her. He was a man broken, and he didn't know what to do to reverse the pain he caused to the only woman who ever showed him any real love. He began to drift off into unconsciousness.

Red pulled his discreet Honda Accord into the small district on the outskirts of Flint, Michigan. It was a small, modest town that was mostly occupied by families of Irish descent. Red wore a skull cap and dark shades as he always did when moving about the city. He had a reputation of robbery and murder and had so many enemies that he couldn't keep count. He always traveled incognito to lower his chances of being spotted. His light, bright skin tone and freckles made him stick out like a sore thumb in any setting. He was pulling up to meet a known gangster by the name of Landon.

Word on the street was that Landon's son was murdered by a young hustler from Flint. This murder rang bells in the ghetto because of who his father was. Shortly after, word got back to Red that Landon wanted a private meeting with him. It was known that Landon was a wealthy owner of a line of grocery stores in the city, but the underground knew that was just a front for his illegal gambling ring.

Red parked his car and looked down at the two pistols that were sitting in his lap. He never went anywhere without his twin pistols. They were almost like accessories for him. It was a part of his daily routine as he got dressed. Red had so many demons that he always thought a past deed would come back knocking at his doorstep. Karma was the most patient gangster ever, and he understood that fully. Red stepped out of the car and entered Landon's place of business. It was a small pub on the corner, a city landmark, and known for more than cheers and beers.

Red walked in, and the pub was empty and quiet. The smell of pine filled Red's nostrils as he hesitantly walked into the establishment. He casually had his hands in his pockets, gripping a pistol in each hand. This was his first meeting with Landon, and he wasn't sure if it was a real thing or a setup. Either way, he was ready for whatever the day may bring.

Only one bartender was present. He was wiping down the counter as the sounds of the midday baseball game sounded from the TV screen mounted on the wall. As soon as Red walked in, the bartender threw his head in the direction of the back office. Red nodded and headed toward the big wooden door, which read OWNER*. As Red approached the door, the bartender walked toward the entrance and quickly flipped the sign from* OPEN *to* CLOSED *and locked the door. Red paused at the sound of the door locking, and he never looked back. He only gripped his pistols tighter. He turned his head, only peeking over his shoulder, and then pushed open the door to find a gigantic office. He took one step in and was greeted by a muscular guy in a gray suit. Red looked up at the man who was well over six feet tall. His hair was slicked back, and he had an unwelcoming grimace on his face. He placed his hand on Red's chest, stopping his progress.*

"I have to check you before you speak to the boss," he said calmly.

"A'ight," Red said as he slid his hands out of his pockets and put them up. He watched as the doorman patted him down and pulled out his twin pistols. Red smirked and had no worries about losing those pieces. He had another smaller-caliber pistol stuffed in the side of his boot for reassurance.

"I'll just hold on to these until you two are done talking," the doorman said as he stepped to the side and exposed the man who sat in a big leather chair.

He was in his late fifties and wore a casual golf shirt and slacks. His eyes were bloodshot and puffy, as if he had been crying. That was because he had been. He had been grieving and hadn't slept in days. He sat behind a cherry-oak desk as cigar smoke hovered over him. The man took a deep pull of the cigar and slowly blew out smoke circles. Red watched closely and walked toward the desk. He stood before him, and they locked eyes. The man behind the desk was none other than Landon.

"Yesterday, I buried my boy. My only son," Landon said as he stood up and reached down into the ashtray to put out the cigar. He walked around the desk and stood face-to-face with Red.

"Okay, so what does that have to do with me?" Red said coldheartedly, wanting to cut the small talk. There was an awkward pause as Landon looked at Red as if he had two heads growing out of his neck.

"Well, you see, not just anyone killed my son. The son of a bitch is connected to Kane Garrett," Landon said as he slammed his fist on his desk, causing a loud thud to echo throughout the office. Red instantly recognized the name. He knew exactly who the man the streets called Kane was. Red nodded his head as he took in the information. He let Landon continue without any interruption.

"The kid's name is Basil. Basil killed my son in the street as if he were a dog, and I want revenge. But you see, in the streets there's a protocol, and I have to follow the rules. I can't just send a mob into Flint to shoot up shit. That will start a war, and that's something nobody wants," Landon said as he stepped closer to Red, now standing eye to eye with him. He continued in almost a whisper. "And that's where you come in, my friend. I need someone who looks like them to get close and avenge my son's death."

Landon was so direct and disrespectful. However, Red wasn't in this game for respect. He was in it for the money. Although Red brushed off Landon's comments, Red knew that he was being used as a pawn. Red instantly thought of how other powerful black men got assassinated in America. It was never their true enemy who murdered them, but always a pawn disguised as their brother. Red began to think about how Malcolm X was killed and then, more recently, Nipsey Hussle. Their killers were mere, meaningless chess pieces dressed in black and brown skin. Red shook his head in disgust but continued to inquire more. He blocked out all morality and sought out a payday.

"How much does it pay? Let's talk numbers," Red said, cutting through the small talk.

Landon smiled and reached over to his desk. He picked up a small piece of paper and showed it to Red. It had a number written on it, and Red's eyes were as big as golf balls. It was a number that he had never seen before in his whole career as a hitter. His mouth instantly began to salivate. His dick began to harden. His brain began to race, thinking about the money that would be in his palms after the hit was done. He could hardly contain his joy as an involuntary smile spread across his face.

"I have all the information on this piece of shit. I have an inside guy on their team who gave me the entire rundown. We know where he likes to visit, what building his stash is in, and the car he drives. We know that he loves to go onto the rooftop with his girl some nights. He runs the Southside Regency projects. That's where you can hit him," Landon said as his jaws began to tighten as he spoke. The anger was building, and the hatred for the man who killed his son was soul deep. Landon then reached into his back pocket and pulled out a white envelope. It was bulky and obviously filled with money. "This is a small advance. The rest—" Landon started but was cut off by Red.

"Say no more. I'll take the hit," Red said, taking the envelope and stuffing it in his pocket. Red knew exactly

who Basil was and was aware of his status. Basil was the king of the streets and had elevated in the game to become the number one guy. Red didn't give a fuck about any of that. The only thing he saw were those zeros and the comma on the paper that Landon had shown him.

Red had laser focus and already began making plans for his big payday. This was going to fund his ghetto retirement. It would be a thug holiday and an exit wound for one of the best who had ever done it. Red turned away and began to walk toward the door. "I'll be back soon to pick up the rest of my paper," he added just before walking over to the doorman. He waited for him to return his guns. The doorman looked over at his boss and waited for the nod of approval, and when he got it, he gave Red back his belongings. Just like that, Red was gone out the door with a new target—a target that would alter his life forever.

Red had been following Basil for a few weeks, and he felt that on that particular night, he would have the best chance to kill him. He watched as Basil partied and drank champagne at some sort of ball or political party. Red had followed Basil for the entire day and watched closely, waiting for a good time to make his attempt. He had never followed a mark for this extended amount of time. However, the big payday was well worth it.

This is my exit wound, *Red thought as he imagined the money bag in his hands. He could finally move away and spend the rest of his life as a regular citizen rather than the coldhearted killer he had become. Red vowed to become the man he had been promising Shawna he would be. She was his sole motivation, which made the hit the grandest of them all.*

Red was about to kill the street's king. He followed Basil back to his stomping ground in the projects. Red sat in the projects' parking lot and stalked his prey. Basil was laughing and drinking on the rooftop with a young lady. Red looked over to his younger goon he occasionally used for hits, and he spoke to him.

"That nigga off his square tonight, young'un. It's time to get paid. We gon' hit him as soon as he come down the fire escape. He parked his car around back, so that's where we gon' catch him slipping," Red instructed as he glanced over at the kid. The kid's name was Harry, and he was a local pill head who stayed high on some sort of drug at all times. Red could tell that Harry was high as a kite. However, Red didn't care because he knew that when it was time to get busy, Harry didn't freeze up. Red focused back on the roof and noticed that Basil had disappeared.

"Okay, that's our cue," Red said as he rolled down his mask and reached in the back seat, grabbing his AK-47. His eyes were piercing under the mask, and he stared at Harry to make sure he was ready. Harry had the eye of the tiger. Red grinned as he winked at his young killer.

"Show time. Let's get it," Harry said as he popped a pill like a mint and rolled down his black ski mask, gripping the semi-automatic weapon that was in his lap.

They both simultaneously slid out of the car and gently closed the car doors. In unison, they trotted across the parking lot with their weapons held to their side to conceal them as best they could. They crept around back where a truck was parked. It was a dark alley that only had a single light above the exit door, barely illuminating the space. It was a perfect setting for Red and his goon to lie in the shadows without being noticed.

Without saying a word, Red instructed Harry to kneel down behind the dumpster that was across from the current one he was at. They had done jobs like this countless times, so it was like clockwork to them. They moved as if they had military training and precision. Harry hurried over and kneeled down as they prepared to take care of business.

The faint sounds of laughter and clatters of hard-bottomed shoes approached the exit door. Red and Harry both gripped their guns and prepared to let off rounds to complete the hit. They watched as the door swung open and out came Basil, carrying a young woman in his arms. Harry's eyes shot over to Red. Red shook his head no, calling off Harry. He knew that it would be impossible to hit Basil without killing the girl in his arms. Red was a coldhearted killer. However, he only intended to kill his target and not the girl.

Basil looked around as he held the woman in his arms, and he saw there was no one in the dark alley. Well, at least that was what he thought.

Basil never saw that he was walking into a trap. He was too focused on the young woman in his arms. He helped her into his truck and then walked over to the driver side and got in. Basil started up the car, and that was when Red and Harry hopped out and swooped over to the driver's side. Bullets began to crash through the glass, and the sounds of shots being fired and glass shattering serenaded the airwaves. The sound of screeching tires erupted, and smoke from the burning rubber of the truck's tires filled the alley. The vehicle wildly sped off, all while Red continued to empty his clip into the car. Harry's gun jammed as he tried to let out his rounds. The truck disappeared out of the parking lot, leaving a trail of dust and smoke dancing in the air.

"Let's go!" Red said hastily as he threw his head in the direction of the getaway car, and like clockwork, they both ran over. They both hopped into the car and sped off.

"Damn, my joint jammed the fuck up. I let him get away," Harry said as he shook his head in disappointment.

"Don't worry, I hit him at least ten times in the chest. He probably on the side of the road taking his last breath," Red said with a sinister smirk on his face as he maneuvered through the back streets. The smell of gun smoke filled the car, and the hit couldn't have been sweeter in Red's mind. He was out of the game for good.

"That's what the fuck I'm talking about!" Red screamed as the adrenaline pumped through his veins. He gripped the steering wheel tightly, and he hit it repeatedly in celebration as he smiled. Red's heart pounded, and the inside of his chest began to tingle. In all his days, he had never celebrated like that.

Red looked over at Harry, who began to go into a nod. The pill had kicked in, and Harry was struggling to keep his eyes open. Red shook his head in disgust and murmured under his breath, "Dopehead," as he kept the grin on his face. Red cleared the neighborhood by a few blocks, and then he slowed down and reached into the armrest for his cell phone. He had to call and let his lady know that the mission was complete. He quickly scrolled through his phone and smiled when he saw his girl's name. He quickly FaceTimed her and waited to see his beauty on the other end.

"Hey, daddy," Shawna said as she sat up in a bed full of rose petals while wearing nothing but a silk gown. She had on a face full of makeup, and her hair was pulled back neatly. She had music playing in the background and was sipping wine, waiting for her man to come home. Her red lipstick and big, bright smile instantly sent a warm feeling through Red's chest. He watched as she held up a wineglass and took a sip. She had been waiting for that video call all night.

"We did it, baby. It's over," Red assured her as he switched his focus from the road to the small phone screen.

"We did it?" Shawna repeated to confirm what she had just heard.

"Yes, it's over. I'm heading over to pick up the bag and then heading home to you," Red said as he felt his voice begin to shake. He knew that his run was over. It was the first time in a very long while that he felt relief. Red looked into the phone as Shawna's breast peeked out of the top of her lingerie. He couldn't wait to get home and make love to his nymphomaniac.

"You are my king, and tonight we are going to make love and celebrate! I got something for you," Shawna said as she slowly lowered the phone, exposing her neatly shaved vagina.

Red's eyes were glued to the phone, and he admired the voluptuous body. As Red's eyes fixated on his girl's prize, he unknowingly veered left, crossing the lane and yellow lines. He was now in the lane of the oncoming traffic. Red licked his lips and smiled as he stared. He didn't even see what was to come. The only thing he heard was the sound of a loud horn, and then bright lights shone directly into his vehicle. He tried to swerve back over into his own lane, but it was too late.

"Noooo!" Red yelled as he instinctively threw up both of his hands to protect himself as he crashed into a smaller car head-on. A loud, horrific, bone-crushing crash erupted, followed by the sounds of squealing tires and screams. The blare of shattered glass and metal crunching resonated through the air. Red's airbags exploded and instantly broke his nose from the impact, nearly knocking him unconscious. Harry never saw it coming. He was halfway into his nod and had a rude awakening. Both cars slammed into each other then violently spun

out of control. Fortunately, they were the only two cars on the road, and it was just that one collision in the car accident. Large pieces from the windshield were deeply embedded into Red's face. Blood profusely gushed down his face. Red barely clung to consciousness.

"Baby, baby! Baby, answer me!" a voice shouted. It was the only thing helping Red to stay awake. The screaming and concerned voice of Shawna was keeping him alive. She screamed through the cell phone as she frantically wondered what had just happened.

Red shook his head, trying to snap out of the daze and regain his vision. With blurred and doubled vision, Red glanced over at Harry. Harry had hit his head against the window, and blood was running from his temple and out of his left ear.

"You good?" Red asked in an exasperated whisper. He blinked rapidly, trying to see through his bloodied eyelids. The smell of the smoking engine and the stench of blood filled the car.

"Yeah, I'm okay. What the fuck happened?" Harry asked as he tried to make sense of what had occurred.

Red was lightheaded and began to feel himself drifting toward sleep. Only the sounds of Shawna's voice kept him present. "Baby! Are you okay? Answer me!" she yelled as she frantically searched for answers.

Red tried to turn his head and felt the weight of the world as he attempted to do so. It seemed as if his head weighed a ton as he let out a painful grunt. Red managed to look in the back seat and saw Shawna's face on the phone's screen. He grabbed it and looked into the camera. The way that Shawna's face looked when she saw Red's appearance was devastating. Shawna instantly began to cry hysterically, which made Red peek into the rearview mirror to look at himself. That's when he saw all of the glass chunks sticking in his face. It seemed like something out of a horror film.

"Yeah, I'm okay. I hit someone, baby. I'm fucked up. I'm fucked up bad," he said as he tried his best to refocus and stop his head from spinning.

"Listen to me closely. Focus on me," Shawna said, knowing the severity of what was going on. She knew that cops would be on the scene shortly and he had murder weapons in the car with him.

"Okay," he said faintly, blinking his eyes slowly and slowly swaying while his head was spinning.

"Red! Stay with me! You have to get yourself together and get the fuck out of there. The police will be there soon," Shawna pleaded. "Please, baby, leave now!"

Reality hit Red all at once as he dropped the phone and realized what was at stake. He had two illegal assault weapons in the car and an open-and-shut murder charge waiting for him if the police came. Red gathered himself and glanced over at the car that was totaled and in a ditch. He quickly focused back on the busted steering wheel with a loose airbag hanging out of it. The airbag had deflated and looked like a dirty laundry bag. Red quickly started the car with his bloody hands. After a few seconds of hesitation, the engine started. Red wrapped his hands around what was left of the steering wheel and drove off. He glanced over as he passed the ditch and saw that the car began to catch fire. He floored the gas pedal as the sounds of police sirens approached. Red's car tires screeched as he faded into the darkness of the night, heading to their safe house.

Chapter Eleven

Shawna stood in the doorway and looked at Red, who was still knocked out cold. She sipped the coffee and wondered how she'd gotten into the position she was in. She wasn't new to the street life, but she was never actually the one doing the crime. Being a girlfriend to a criminal and being the actual criminal were two completely different things.

Shawna couldn't believe she was in a stranger's house, holding him against his will, all for the love of a man, a man she wasn't even sure still loved her. A faint pain shot through her heart as she stared at Red as he lay there snoring. She wanted his love so badly that she'd compromised herself. Shawna was desperately trying to find the old Red, but she somehow had lost herself in the process. Tears began to well up in her eyes as she kept replaying the harsh words that Bless had said to her. Although Red wasn't the easiest to deal with, he never put his hands on her or verbally abused her before the accident.

Shawna was so in love with the idea of being in love, she would live through hell attempting to regain that feeling. It wasn't until Bless pointed it out that she saw it from a bird's-eye view. As her tears began to flow, the harsh reality began to sink in. Shawna leaned against the wall and slid to the ground, landing on her butt. She cried like a baby, letting out all of her emotions. Somehow, she realized that the old Red was no more. Shawna missed her man so much, and her heart ached for attention.

She hadn't made love in so long, and she couldn't even remember the last time she saw Red smile at her. He had barely complimented her in any capacity, and it had her doubting her own beauty, something that she had never done before.

Red turned slightly, getting more comfortable as he slept. Shawna quickly wiped her tears away and stood up, not wanting him to see her crying. Once she saw that he was still asleep, she exited the room and reentered the living room, where Bless was tied up. Shawna had managed to wipe all her tears away and looked at the clock and saw that it was approaching 6:00 a.m. The sun had just begun to come up, and she was exhausted. Shawna glanced over at Bless, and he was looking at her as she walked toward the coffee pot in the kitchen.

"I need to use the restroom," Bless said as he looked through his cracked lens.

"Restroom?" Shawna asked as she turned around and fully faced Bless. "I don't know what you're telling me for. You betta piss on yourself, because I'm not untying you," Shawna said as she placed her hands on her hips and snaked her neck as she spoke.

"You don't just expect me to piss on myself, do you? Like really?" Bless asked as he shook his head in disbelief. "Can I at least piss in the plant?" he requested as he threw his head in the direction of the three-foot-tall leafy plant that sat off in the corner.

Shawna glanced over to the plant and realized that would be a better option than babysitting a pissy hostage. She rolled her eyes and walked over to the plant and picked it up. She placed it right next to Bless and said, "There you go. Do your thing." She looked at Bless and grinned.

"I'm good, but I'm not that good. I need to pull it out. My hands are tied as you can see," Bless said as he threw his head in the direction of his tied hands, which were behind his back.

Shawna looked down at Bless's crotch area and couldn't help but notice the bulge. Shawna didn't want to stare, but she had to. She noticed his girth, and it instantly made her feel a way. She tried to look away, but for some reason she just couldn't. Shawna instantly felt her clitoris begin to lightly thump. She involuntarily placed her hand on her chest and began to breathe deeply.

Bless noticed her sudden hot flash and spread his legs a bit more so she could get a better angle. "Can you pull it out for me?" he asked.

With everything in her, Shawna wanted to feel offended, but she didn't at all. Her eyes didn't leave his growing bulge. Although she didn't want to, she wanted to see how it looked. She hadn't seen a nice one in so long, and her addiction began to show its ugly head. Shawna slowly felt her hand begin to drift down toward his pants. Before she knew it, her hand was wrapped around his thick pole, and instantly her nipples began to harden thinking about how it felt to have a stiff one inside of her. Shawna had been getting a limp noodle for so long she'd actually forgotten how it felt.

Just in those few seconds, her panties got soaked. They were literally dripping with her juices, and she could begin to feel the wetness on her inner thighs. Shawna ran her hand over his base and then crept up the pole while gently squeezing it. She could literally see the veins through his Italian cloth material. It began to grow in her hand. She thought about what she was doing and quickly yanked her hand back and stepped back. Shawna put her hand over her mouth, and shame overcame her as she realized what she had done without thinking. Bless looked at her but remained silent for a moment.

"It's been that long?" he asked almost as if he were reading her mind and knew her struggle. Shawna couldn't believe it, but something inside of her was pushing her to respond. She slowly nodded her head, confirming his inquiry. He slowly nodded as well, almost as if he was comforting her nonverbally. Even through his cracked lenses, Shawna felt like Bless was looking directly into her soul. Shawna felt a warm feeling she hadn't felt in a long time.

Bless sincerely seemed like he cared, and she didn't notice how much she needed that until she felt it from another man. Although Bless had a nerdy vibe, his eyes said something different, and Shawna was beginning to feel it.

"I'm sorry I got excited," Bless whispered as he looked down at his pipe, which was fully erect and literally trying to bust out of his pants. He grew a self-conscious look on his face and shook his head in embarrassment. "I just haven't been with a woman in so long, and I got carried away. You're so beautiful, and I honestly couldn't help it," Bless admitted.

Shawna smiled even though she didn't want to. She was craving attention. Shawna hadn't heard she was beautiful in so long that she began to doubt her self-worth.

"Can I tell you something else?" Bless asked as he mentally began to peel layers back from the mind of the lady who acted as his capturer. Shawna was wide open, and he could tell. Her eyes were different from before. She was desperately anticipating his next words. It was selfish but she needed it. No, she yearned for it. Shawna nodded her head, urging him to go on.

"It's not going to get better. I see the way he looks at you. That's not love," Bless admitted.

"It's that obvious?" Shawna asked as she squinted her eyes, trying to understand what Bless saw that she hadn't.

"Yes, it is. I'm not sure how it used to be, but I can see that it's different now. Sometimes . . ." Bless spoke softly and paused mid-sentence. He checked the hallway to make sure Red wasn't coming so he could lay the whole truth on her. Bless continued once he saw that the coast was clear. "Sometimes a woman holds on to a man for what he used to be. She is so desperate to restore that old feeling that she sacrifices the now and loses herself in the process. Ultimately the 'now' ends up being the rest of her life. That's no way to live. Does this make sense?" Bless asked.

She nodded as she felt as if she were getting a word from God through the lips of Bless.

"That's why I really miss my lady. We had gotten through all the bullshit, and we were still standing. I was at a point of my life where I understood her worth, and she knew that I understood it. I worked so hard to get to that point, and then . . ." Bless said as his eyes began to mist over.

"She died?" Shawna whispered as she hung on his every word.

Bless nodded in confirmation. "Yes, she died from a rare case of cancer a few years back," Bless said as a tear dropped, landing in his lap.

"I'm so sorry," Shawna said as she put her hand over her mouth. A sudden wave of tremendous guilt had overcome her. Red's and her greed had made them target a man who was already going through hell. He was fighting an internal battle just like she had been. They both had lost their loved ones and were trying to figure out that thing called life again. Bless was a broken man, and it was written all over his face.

"Oh, my God, you really loved her. Didn't you?" Shawna asked, realizing what true love looked like. It looked like pain. She could see the pain written all over Bless. In a twisted way, she just wanted to help Bless. Shawna knew that he needed love just as she did.

In her sexually driven mind, the vulnerability of Bless made her pussy even wetter. She didn't usually like nerds, but there was something about his vulnerability and his ability to understand her that drove her hormones crazy. Shawna wanted him, and she wanted him now.

She tossed the gun onto the couch near her and focused back on Bless. She slowly walked toward him, and they just stared into each other's eyes as if they were sharing their pain with one another. She moved the plant over with her leg and then hovered just above Bless. She slightly parted her legs.

"Can I . . ." Shawna stopped in mid-sentence, not wanting to say what she really wanted.

"You want to sit on it, don't you?" Bless whispered as he looked up and into her eyes.

She nodded her head, verifying his notion. Bless was tied up, but he was the one in complete control.

Shawna's hand slowly slid down to her love box. Her hand lightly brushed up against her clitoris, making her knees buckle slightly. Her eyes involuntarily closed, and a small, lustful moan escaped her lips. She slowly pulled up her skirt, revealing her lace panties, and it immediately gave Bless a full erection. His tool was so hard that it hurt. Shawna reached down to unzip his pants. She reached into his slacks and pulled out the most delicious dick she had ever seen. Her mouth began to salivate.

Bless was a dark man, and his tool seemed to be two shades darker than his complexion. His thickness overwhelmed her, and she could see the long, thick vein that ran from his base to the beginning of his tip.

Shawna looked at the pulsating, fat tip. It looked like a bloomed mushroom head, and it was the prettiest dick she had ever seen in her life. It wasn't super long, but the thickness and bulging veins drove her crazy. It sat on top of his ball sack, and the only thing she could think about was sucking it. Shawna imagined it filling her mouth and brushing up against the sides of her cheeks.

Shawna ran her tongue across her top lip and breathed deeply as some of her juices dripped on Bless's knee, causing a wet spot to form on his pants. She wanted to suck it so badly, but she knew that she was playing with fire and couldn't waste any time. There was no time for foreplay. She wanted to feel it in the worst way. Red could enter the room at any second, and that would be the death of both of them.

Although no one was touching it, Bless's rod swayed back and forth as it stood straight up, pointed directly at Shawna. It was as if it had a mind of its own. Bless's eyes were fixated on her love box and the small tattoo that was just to the left it. Shawna reached down and slid her panties to the side as she mounted him. He slid in with ease. The sound of her wetness was as if someone were stirring creamy pasta. Shawna sat all the way down on it as she wrapped her arms around Bless's neck. She slowly began to move her hips in circular motions, crashing down on his lap with every cycle. Their rhythm was in complete unison.

Bless did his best to thrust his hips into her every single time. He plunged into her love over and over. They both were in much need of a sexual release. After a minute of nonstop thrusting, both Bless and Shawna felt a climax brewing. They both were whispering how good it felt to one another, and they stared into each other's eyes as she bounced up and down on him vigorously. Shawna rode harder and faster as she felt an explosion coming.

She put her hand over her mouth to muffle the scream that she knew was approaching. She closed her eyes and continued to bounce, and she felt her love coming down. Her legs began to shake, and her body convulsed feverishly as she let it all go.

Shawna felt a gush of fluid shoot from her vagina, and it left her temporarily dazed. At that point, she didn't have any control over her body's movements, and she quivered like she had never done before. The squirting took her by surprise and, to be honest, Bless too. She sat completely down and just jerked violently for a few seconds as she continued to leak all over Bless. He was touching the bottom of her love box, and he just sat there as she tried to regain her composure. Her eyes were rolling behind her head, and incoherent gibberish was coming from her mouth.

After gathering herself, Shawna stood up and Bless slid out of her. She looked down and his entire lap was soaked. She quickly put his penis back in his pants for him, and the feeling of guilt washed over her. Shawna knew she was wrong, but her body's desire got the best of her. She fell victim to her temptation. Although she regretted it, it was hands-down the best orgasm she'd ever had by far. Shawna was speechless as she pulled down her skirt and stepped away, walking awkwardly. She looked at Bless, and he couldn't look her in the eye, and at that moment, she knew that he was ashamed of what he had done as well.

"I know . . ." Bless whispered as Shawna was moving away from him.

"Know what?" Shawna asked as she was confused by his random comment.

"I know that Fonz is your brother," he admitted.

Shawna's heart dropped as she didn't understand how he knew. She instantly got scared, knowing that their cover was blown and Bless knew about the setup. At that point, she began to think about her freedom and what she had gotten herself into.

"What the fuck are you talking about?" she asked, trying to play dumb. Shawna didn't want to blow her cover and expose her brother for the play he had orchestrated.

"I saw your tattoo. It says Linwood. That's the same tattoo on Fonz's neck. You guys are from the same neighborhood. To be honest, I didn't understand how you guys knew my business, but now it makes sense. I was talking business in front of Fonz, and he caught it," Bless said in a humble tone. He was beating himself up on the inside for being so careless. Bless shook his head in disappointment of himself as thoughts began to flood his mind. He understood that he had brought this stickup on himself. Bless dropped his head and shook it in defeat.

"That's nonsense. I never heard of a nigga named Fonzi or Fonzo. Whatever the fuck name you said," Shawna lied, trying to stay true to character.

"I don't have a lot of people in my life, so I know where the leak came from. You don't have to deny it. I know I'm not the toughest, and it seems like I was an easy target. I get it," Bless explained as he looked into Shawna's eyes, trying to read her.

"You bugging, my nigga. You're wrong," she said.

"Your mother is very sick. She's dying of cancer, correct?" Bless asked.

Shawna didn't say anything, but his words were like daggers to her heart. Her mother was indeed dying, and that was a sore spot for her because it was an inevitable fate that she was dealing with. Shawna wanted to keep denying it, but the pain of her mother's illness was heavy on her heart. Bless saw the pain in her face and continued.

"I can see it all over your face, love. Fonz slipped and mentioned you to me before, and then Red said your name earlier. Shawna, right?" Bless said matter-of-factly.

"No," she whispered. A tear slid down her face as she thought about her dying mom.

"Listen, remember the help that your mom got? The medical attention, the homecare nurse, the new bed. I did that. I gave Fonz the money to do that because I felt his pain. I was empathetic toward him," Bless explained carefully. "Just let me go. Return the favor, and show me some empathy."

"I can't," Shawna said with heavy uncertainty.

"You know and I know that the man in there is not in his right mind. After he gets the money, he is going to kill me to cover his tracks. I don't deserve this. Please just give me a chance," Bless advised.

"Red would never forgive me if he knew I let you go. He would kill me," Shawna said as her voice shook in fear.

"We can do this. I can save you from that madman in the room. If you let me go, I will come and get you from him. This is your only way out, to be honest. He is a crazed man. Once he gets the money, he is going to become a bigger monster. Money doesn't change people. It just makes them more of the person they really are. You have to listen to me. You have to trust me. He doesn't love you, Shawna," Bless pleaded.

Shawna's hand began to shake as she reached for the gun. She had been exposed, and she didn't like the feeling. She didn't know what to do. She thought that it was Fonz who had helped their mother with the medical things, and now she'd come to find out it was Bless. Bless had helped her mother's quality of life. This just made her feel horrible. It really made a difference with her mom to have that newfound comfort, and she was standing there holding a gun on the man responsible for it. They had taken advantage of a gentle man, and the guilt was becoming unbearable.

"I can't let you go. Red will kill me if he finds out," she pleaded.

Bless had all her walls down at that point. He had broken through to her, and it was evident. Bless paused and thought about what he was about to say before he said it. "Listen, just untie me and let me escape. I will hit you and give you a bruise so it looks good. You can say you let me use the bathroom and I attacked you just before running out. Come on, beautiful. Please do this for me."

"He won't believe it," Shawna said in an exasperated whisper as she looked back toward the back room to make sure Red wasn't coming. He would be up at any moment now, because she knew the medicine would begin to wear off.

"You have to trust me. If you don't do this, he is going to kill me. Just do the right thing."

Shawna swiftly nodded her head while Bless was talking, going along with his instructions. She was spiraling downward with Red and was unhappy. Bless had given her an exit plan that had never been presented to her before. She was tired of living the street life, and Bless seemed like her knight in shining armor.

"Come here," Bless said to her. Shawna slowly walked over to him and breathed heavily as she stood over him. "Closer," he whispered as he licked his lips. Shawna leaned down, now face-to-face with him. Bless stuck out his tongue, and Shawna leaned forward. They began to kiss, and the mere passion of Bless sent tingles down Shawna's spine, making her clitoris thump. Her body reacted to him organically. "Do it for me," he whispered as he looked deep into her eyes.

"Okay," she whispered as she set down the gun and began to untie him. After a few seconds, she had loosened the binding, and he was finally free.

Bless quickly held his arms in front of him and rubbed the raw skin where the binding was around his wrist. His skin was raw and red. He placed his hand on the back of his neck and stretched it out, seeking comfort from the hours of the uncompromising position he'd been in.

Bless leaned forward and gently grabbed Shawna by the face, palming both of her cheeks. He slowly kissed her forehead, and then he went lower to kiss her lips. "Thank you," he whispered as he pulled back from the kiss and looked into her eyes. She put her hands over his and felt safe for the first time in a very long while.

"Okay, I'm going to hit you, and then I'm going to run out. Wait a few second, and then go wake him up. I'll be long gone before he even has a chance to come after me. Come back here after a week or so, and I will take care of the rest. Let's build," Bless said in confidence, laying out the entire play for her. He left her no room for doubt. He spoke precisely and confidently, which gave her confidence.

"Okay, okay," Shawna whispered as she stepped back and closed her eyes. She took a deep breath and prepared for Bless to strike her. He held his hand up and prepared to strike her. She closed her eyes and braced for impact. Bless paused with his hand in the air and then lowered his hand.

"I can't. I just can't," Bless said as he shook his head no. "I'm just going to leave," he said as he kissed her on the forehead and then took off toward the front door.

He ran to the front door and stopped just as he got to it. Bless placed his hand on the door and paused. He took a deep breath and punched in a code on the keypad that was just left of the door. Moments later there were sounds of deadbolts and multiple clicks. The windows throughout the house shut with steel bars ascending from the windowsills. The house was going into a complete lockdown thanks to the advanced security system.

Bless took off his glasses and tossed them on the floor. He then reached over to the plant and lifted it up. A pistol with a silencer was hidden under it, and he picked it up. He began to peel off his shirt so he could get more comfortable. Bless slowly exposed his chiseled body and many tattoos. He stood upright and walked with confidence. He walked into the living room where Shawna stared at the windows, wondering what was happening.

She was confused and didn't expect to see Bless walk back in. He looked different without his glasses, and he seemed to have a different look in his eyes from before. Bless pointed the gun at her as they locked eyes. Shawna didn't know what to say. She watched as he picked her gun up from the floor. Bless placed it in the small of his back and had a deranged look on his face.

Red came from the back room groggy and confused. The sounds of the windows locking throughout the house woke him up, and he had no idea what was going on. He walked out to see the shirtless Bless, who was pointing a gun at the head of his woman.

"What took you so long? I've been waiting for so long to find yo' bitch ass," Bless snarled. Even his voice was different. It was deeper, and his diction had completely changed. It wasn't as proper and polished as before.

"Wait. Wait. Hold on," Red said as he held his hands in front of him, trying to plead.

"Nah, my nigga. I've waited long enough. I been looking for you and couldn't seem to find you. After the accident you disappeared. It was like you dropped off the face of the mu'fuckin' earth. So I had to bring yo' ass out of hiding. I had to use bait," Bless said with a menacing smirk on his face.

"What are you talking about, G? Put down the gun. I'll leave right now," Red pleaded as he tried to make sense of what was going on.

"Nah, you not going anywhere. You stuck in this bitch. See, I'm not who you think I am. I'm Bless, my nigga. I blessed the streets. Been doing it for years. I'm not the square you thought I was. Sadly you were misinformed. I want to explain something to you. See if you can remember. . . ."

Bless sat at the table and looked down at his lobster and shrimp linguini as the speaker stood at the podium. A live band was playing jazz, and a beautiful black queen stood center stage with a microphone and smoothly scatted to the rhythm of the beat. Bless was at a mayor's ball to finalize a deal between him and his new distributor. He looked across the table at his lady, who was eating as well. She was stunning, as she had her hair neatly pulled back into a bun, and her makeup was done to perfection. It wasn't too much, but it was just enough to highlight her beauty. Her diamond studs shone in the light, and he just smiled at her as she slurped a long noodle into her mouth. She looked up and caught him staring and instantly made her eyes look crossed, causing both of them to burst into laughter. Bless loved to see his leading lady smiling and having a good time. He was staring at the love of his life and wife, Queen. She had accompanied him to Flint to attend the party of his coke connect, Basil. He invited Queen because they hadn't had a chance to dress up in formal attire since their high school prom. It warmed his heart to see his wife radiate beauty like she did that night. Her all-white ballroom gown made Queen look like an angel in his eyes. The mink shawl around her shoulders was icing on the cake. Bless admired her beauty as they shared the laugh together.

Bless heard someone call his name from afar and looked up to see his big homie Kane Garrett calling him over. Kane Garrett was what the streets called "old money." Kane was a street legend who'd made his name an urban myth. He wasn't the mayor of the City of Flint, but he might as well have been, because he had all the politicians in his back pocket. Bless excused himself from the table and walked over to Kane, who was standing with Basil.

"Peace, Kane," Bless greeted him.

Kane put one arm around each of the two men next to him and began to talk. "You two are the future of this thing. This invite was not so much a celebration but more of an introduction. To truly have power, you have to have a firm hand in politics. If I knew this earlier, I would have never gone to prison, because I would've had every judge in the state in my pocket. I set up a golf outing between us and a senator in the morning. I need both of you there. Got it?" Kane stated. Both of them nodded in agreement, knowing that they were getting put in position to acquire real power.

"Absolutely," Bless said. Basil nodded his head in agreement as well.

"Good," Kane said as he patted both of their backs. Kane saw a friend across the floor and proceeded to leave them there alone to talk. They both watched as Kane walked away and then began their own conversation. They slapped hands and embraced before they began their dealings.

"We still good for tonight?" Bless asked as he moved the toothpick around that was in his mouth. He also did that move just in case someone was watching and could read lips.

"Yes, sir. You got a hunnid of 'em in the trunk. Blue Honda Civic," Basil said as he reached into his pocket and dangled a set of car keys in front of Bless. Bless held out his hand, and the keys were dropped into his palm.

"Outside?" Bless asked, surprised.

"Outside in the parking lot. Last row," Basil assured him.

"My nigga," Bless said as a huge smile spread across his face. Bless thought that they were meeting there to discuss the deal, not actually put it into action. However, he wasn't complaining, not one bit. They slapped hands and shared a quick embrace. Bless was excited because he knew that he was about to make it snow in Detroit.

"I'll be back to get you together in a week or so," Bless whispered in his ear while they were embracing.

"Say no more," Basil answered, knowing that Bless was a reliable business partner. Bless walked over to the table where Queen was, and he reached out his hand to her.

"May I have this dance?" Bless asked as he waited for her to accept. She looked at him like he was crazy, and she began to smile from ear to ear. She placed her hand on her chest and paused a beat.

"I would love to," Queen said in her most prim and proper voice. She stood up and followed him onto the dance floor. Bless took her into his arms and held her closely. He was smiling as he was staring into her eyes. Queen grinned and jerked her head to the side, squinting her eyes.

"Negro, why are you cheesing like that? And why are you dancing? You don't dance," Queen quizzed while enjoying every second of it.

"I just feel good and want to dance with my woman," Bless said as he continued to sway back and forth.

"You just made a play, didn't you?" Queen asked, knowing her man like the back of her hand. Bless was the most stoic gangster she had ever met, and he rarely danced or even smiled in public for that matter. He paused and looked at her but knew that she could see right through him as she always did.

"A hundred of 'em," he whispered as he leaned forward and put his lips right by her ear. He then began to rock

again, placing his hand on her lower back, guiding her to catch his groove.

"My nigga," Queen said as she chuckled and laid her head on his chest. She loved that man so much. She loved him to her core, and they had reached a certain point where everything was blissful. They not only loved one another, but they trusted each other fully. If you know anything about a true union, loyalty and trust is the final level of eternal love. They were both at that point, and love never felt better. They danced and laughed with each other for a few songs before deciding to stop. Bless then instructed her to head home so he could drive the other car to his trap spot. He told Queen that he would meet her home later that night.

Bless walked Queen out to their car and saw her off. He opened the door for her and watched as she sat in the car and started it up. He gently kissed her forehead and told her that he loved her.

"I love you too, Bless. Forever and a day," she added just before closing the door. She rolled down the window and looked at her man.

"Call me when you get home to let me know that you made it," Bless instructed her, and he gently tapped the roof of the car.

"Sure will," Queen said as she looked at him and smiled. Bless watched as his wife exited the parking lot, and when she got out of his view, he made a phone call. He dialed up a member of his crew to let him know that the bag was in.

"Go time. Meet me at the spot," he said quickly just before hanging up the phone. He ended the call and slid the phone into his pocket. He walked over to the blue Honda Civic and hit the unlock button. He drove the opposite way of his wife, heading toward his spot so he could drop off the goods.

Queen grooved to the R&B music as she slowly danced in her seat to the beat. She turned onto a two-lane highway heading home, just like Bless told her to. As she began to sing along to the music, she saw the bright lights of an oncoming car, and she tried to swerve out of the way, but it was too late. Queen had no chance. The oncoming truck was going over eighty miles per hour and merged into her lane, hitting her head-on. The truck smashed into hers, causing her smaller car to be crushed like a tuna can. The impact was so violent that the engine was shoved into her chest and crushed her legs, pelvic area, and sternum. Her car spun and flipped into a ditch. Her entire life flashed before her eyes as she swallowed blood, desperately trying to catch her breath. However, it was to no avail. Queen was dying. Thoughts of her and Bless laughing and dancing crossed her mind as blood filled her lungs, suffocating her slowly. Her eyes were wide open as the last movie she would ever see flashed in her thoughts. Queen was thinking of the love of her life, Bless. She began to breathe slower. Her breathing became slow and shallow until it eventually stopped. Queen was dead. She died alone. She died afraid. She died a horrible death. The streets had no Queen. She was no more.

Tears were falling from Bless's eyes as he relived that painful night when he got the phone call that his wife had been in a terrible car accident.

"You see, I have been trying to find you ever since. You got low, and nobody knew where you were. I put money on your head, but no one could cash in that ticket. You were my little red fox, and I thought about finding you every second of every day. I retraced your steps, went to your neighborhood, and came up with nothing. You became a fucking ghost. I was obsessed with finding you," Bless said as he pressed his gun firmly onto Shawna's temple as he talked directly to Red.

"Wait, what the fuck?" Red asked, trying to make sense of it all. "That was your wife in that crash?" he asked.

"Yes, you bitch-ass nigga! That was my wife!" Bless yelled as spit flew out of his mouth and a snot bubble came from his nose. He was totally unhinged with rage at that point. "You took her from me! You left her to die on the side of the road with no remorse or cares in the world! You hit her and went about your fuckin' way. You left my baby on the side of the road like a fucking piece of roadkill!" Bless screamed. The thought of her dying all alone made his stomach form knots. Red tried to interject and explain, but Bless cut him off, not wanting to hear a word that came from his mouth.

"Shut the fuck up! You have nothing to say to me!" Bless yelled. He looked over at Shawna, and without hesitation, fired two rounds into her skull, killing her instantly. Red shrieked as he saw his woman's body drop and her lifeless eyes stare into dead space.

"Shawna!" Red screamed as he rushed over to her and cupped her head, which was blown open. Brain matter dripped onto the floor and on his hands. Blood was everywhere, and the foul stench of her defecating on herself filled the room. Red began to cry as he rocked his lady back and forth. At that point, he knew that he was about to die, so he chose to just focus on Shawna's face so it would be the last thing he saw before he met his Maker.

"I finally found my red fox. You fell right into my trap. I never had a lawyer meeting me to drop off money. That was all made up. The only person I ever was expecting was you. And now I have that," Bless said as he walked over to Red and stood directly over him.

Red continued to rock Shawna's lifeless body. He was rubbing her hair, trying to make her look as pretty as he could.

Bless continued talking to Red. “I couldn’t find you, so I used bait and made you come to me. Queen would have been proud,” Bless said. He placed the gun to the back of Red’s head. As Red stared deeply into Shawna’s lifeless eyes, four shots rang out, all to the back of Red’s head, rocking him to sleep forever.

The End

Second Puzzle Piece Complete.

Also available by ***JaQuavis Coleman***

Cubana

Prologue

Duality

Five little monkeys jumping on the bed
One fell off and bumped his head
Mama called the doctor, and the doctor said
No more . . . monkeys . . . jumping on the bed

The young child gleefully sang the lullaby as she smiled, playing patty-cake with her imaginary friend. A little brown girl sat Indian style on the floor, wearing a long, white pajama gown. Her skin was ebony, but her eyes . . . Her eyes were ice-cold blue—a rare combination; however, a beautiful one. Her angelic voice echoed through the sparsely furnished house. Four pigtails hung from her head. She looked to be no older than 6 or 7 years old. She continued to sing the children's song, merrily clapping the air as if there were someone else directly in front of her. The happiness in her eyes was innocent and pure.

The open windows allowed her voice to travel onto the streets of Havana, Cuba. The dilapidated homes lined the block, which sat on a long, dirt road. Stray monkeys hopped around the streets playfully along with kids without a care in the world. The simple, familiar, lullaby was majestic and loud. It was peaceful and highlighted the Sunday morning. Loud enough for the man just outside to hear it as he walked toward the home. He had a small, leather duffle bag in his hand as he made his way toward the house. As the man approached the door, he glanced around and peeked down the block, watching while the kids played stickball in the middle of the street. He also saw young girls jump roping and others playing tag; some of them barefooted. It was a harsh but lovely sight to behold. The blissful adolescents were having so much fun, although they were impoverished, not even being able to afford the bare necessities of a simple pair of shoes. Their innocence wouldn't allow them to understand the extent of their own dire situations.

Some of the houses had openings where windows should have been. Roofs were damaged, and each house looked like it was one strong wind away from collapsing. What the city lacked in wealth, they made up for with pride and tradition. The graffiti-littered surfaces on the side of houses and buildings were ugly but also stunning—duality at its finest.

The man scanned further down the street and saw various domino matches being played at small tables. People congregated outside of some of the homes, laughing and speaking Spanish. Groups of men huddled around the small tables and hooted as the beaming hot sun seemed not to bother their golden skin complexions.

Saint Von was the man's name who scoped the neighborhood. He simply went by Saint. He was visiting from the United States . . . New Orleans, Louisiana, to be exact. Saint felt the burning sun shining down on his neck as he pulled the bucket hat down snugly onto his shiny, bald head. He tried to block the sun from his eyes and then straightened the gold-rimmed sunglasses on his face. A toothpick hung from the left side of his mouth as he twisted it using his thumb and pointer finger. He carried a small duffle bag in the other hand. Sweat beads dripped from his brow as he made his way into the house where the angel-like voice was coming from.

Saint wore an open, white linen shirt, and his tattooed body was on full display as a bulging belly somewhat stuck out over his belt buckle. Saint wasn't flabby by any means, but his belly slightly poked out and served as a trophy for his years of good living. His neatly trimmed, full beard hung down to his Adam's apple, and his bear-like face was highlighted by beautiful white teeth on the top row, with a gold row across the bottom.

Just before he stepped into the doorless home, he heard the sounds of monkeys panting and making noises just above him. It made him look up and notice the wild animals hopping around on the roof of the five-story building next door. They were moving frantically, playfully beating on their chest. He shook his head and entered the home. He couldn't get used to the wild animals blending in with society as if normal. It was a far cry from his upbringing in Nola.

As he stepped inside the house, he saw a dimly lit hall. A creaky flight of stairs was right in front of him that led to the second story of the flat. The long, dim, and damp hall was one that Saint had been in quite a few times. He had made it a habit to come to see the woman they called Pandora every time that he visited Cuba. It was always his last stop before heading back home. As he climbed the stairs, the sound of the child's voice grew louder and louder. The smell of burning incense filled Saint's nostrils as he approached the door at the top of the staircase.

As Saint entered the room, he saw the young girl on the floor, playing. He paused and then smiled as he walked past her. They locked eyes, and Saint's bright smile triggered her to return one as well. He headed toward the back where long, flowing beads separated the rooms as they hung from the door's overpass.

Saint slowly walked into the room. The sound of the beads tapping one another always soothed him. He entered. The deeper he got in the room, the less and less he heard the young girl's voice. He squinted his eyes and tried to focus on the dark figure that was in the corner. As he got closer, he heard the sound of a match being lit, and a large flash of light followed it. The flame was connected to a long, wooden matchstick, which was held by unusually long, manicured nails. Each nail was at least four inches long.

A woman's face appeared as the match's flame slightly illuminated the room. Saint's eyes locked in with hers. Her beautiful, big, penny-shaped pupils and full lips let him know exactly who it was. The familiar face soothed him as he walked closer to the light, exposing her face more clearly. The gorgeous woman before him was none other than Pandora. She wore a multicolored silk wrap around her gray locs, which hung out from the top of it.

"I've been expecting you, Saint," Pandora whispered as a small grin formed on her face. She spoke clear English but with a heavy Spanish accent. Her skin was the deepest ebony Saint had ever seen. Her eyes were a rare blue color. They were oddly gorgeous. In this beautiful country, it was a usual combination; however, the States had stripped Saint's interpretation of what Black looked and sounded like. A Black woman's physical characteristics had limitless shades and mixtures, and Pandora was the evidence of that. He was standing there in pure amazement.

Pandora was simply majestic to the naked eye. She was nearly twenty years his senior. However, one couldn't tell by her looks and smooth skin. It was when she opened her mouth that her age showed. Pure wisdom flowed from her mouth, and the strain in her voice showed her years on this earth. She proceeded to light the candles that were spread around the table where she was sitting as Saint stood before her.

"Have a seat," she instructed as she blew out the match and focused her undivided attention on him.

Saint's eyes followed the smoke from the match, and it led directly into her blue eyes. Her gaze was piercing and unwavering as she stared at him, almost as if she were looking *through* him rather than *at* him. An intense chill crept up his spine, and he felt his shoulders becoming more relaxed at the end of it. A small flutter happened in Saint's heart, and like always, he was mesmerized by her presence. He slowly took a seat and gently set the duffle bag on the hardwood floor next to his chair. Saint placed his hands on his lap and took a deep breath as the smell of burning sage and incense calmed him.

"Hey, Pandora," Saint said, as he got comfortable in his chair and looked around the room.

"Hello, handsome," she said as she strategically spread the small crystals around the table. Saint looked at the little gems as she aligned them and incoherently mumbled things under her breath. Pandora closed her eyes and slowly swayed back and forth, and then she stopped abruptly and froze. A small smile formed on her face, and she opened her eyelids, focusing directly on Saint.

"Our ancestors are ready to speak. But before we do what you came here for, let's talk. I feel something is on your heart. Something other than what's in that bag down there," she said as she nodded her head in the direction of the duffle bag full of plastic-wrapped kilos.

Saint was taken aback because it seemed as if she were reading his mind. He usually would come to get his "bricks baptized" by Pandora. He would ask her to separate any Karma or harm that would come to him by way of the bricks of heroin he was about to distribute back in the United States. However, on this particular trip, he had a few extra things going on in his life that he needed help with.

"Damn, you always seem to know what's on my mind," Saint said, shaking his head in amazement.

"No, I always know what's on your heart. I can see it through your eyes. So . . . Come on, talk to mama," Pandora said as she winked and attempted to lighten the mood. Although Pandora was highly spiritual, she had a way of making people feel comfortable with her. Her motherly spirit was one of comfort. She had a special skill for making people open to her.

"There are a few things. I ran into some legal trouble a few years back, and the case came back up. My trial starts in a few," Saint admitted.

"Oh, I see. You're on trial for what cause?"

"Murder," he answered in a low tone as his eyes dropped, breaking their gaze.

"Did you do it?" Pandora asked blatantly and without hesitation. Saint nodded his head in admittance.

"Yeah, but in self-defense," he whispered, genuinely having regret for what he had done. He had sorrow but not for defending himself. Rather, for taking the life of someone that he knew personally.

"I can see that your words are pure, and you have remorse," Pandora said, as she clasped her hands together. She paused and just stared at Saint before speaking again. You could tell that she was analyzing him and choosing her words wisely before she spoke.

"I will ask for guidance from our ancestors, and if I can help you . . . I will. You will have to come back after the sun sets," Pandora explained carefully. Saint nodded in agreement and reached down to go into his bag and placed his hand on a brick. He was about to put them on the table so Pandora could bless them, but Pandora waved her hand, signaling for him to pause.

"There is something else on your heart. What else is troubling you?" she asked as she rested her hands on top of his. Saint closed his eyes and paused, realizing that he couldn't get anything past her. He took a deep breath and sat upright. He chuckled to himself and shook his head, realizing that Pandora was very good at what she did. He couldn't get anything past her. He slightly showed the golds in his mouth with his partial smile.

"I'm getting married. Well, if I'm not in prison . . . I'll be getting married."

"Ooh, here is the *good* stuff," Pandora said playfully as she sat upright as well. "Do tell . . ." she said.

"There's really nothing to tell. Shorty is the truth. I just don't know if I'll be the man she wants me to be. I never did anything like this before," he honestly admitted.

"Okay, I see. You have cold feet, eh?" Pandora said as she nodded slowly, understanding exactly what was going on. "Well, you need some advice, not divine intervention." Pandora slowly waved her arm across the table, clearing all the stones and gems so it would be a clear pallet. She placed her hands on the table with her palms facing up.

"Come on," she instructed as she glanced down at her hands, wiggled her fingers, and then looked up at Saint. Saint placed his hands inside of hers and listened carefully, knowing that she was about to lay some game on him as she always did.

"What's your worries, Saint? Do you not love her?" Pandora asked.

"Of course, I love her. She's a real one," he admitted.

"So, if she's the one . . . Why the hesitation?"

"That's the million-dollar question. I don't know exactly. I dream about her in colors that don't exist." He paused as he let his words marinate. "She's been there with me from the beginning. I just want to reward her with everything. She deserves to be happy. She has been through it all. She held me down every single time and never once made me think she wasn't in my corner. Even when it was hard," Saint said, feeling the urge to tell Pandora every single emotion he was feeling toward his fiancée.

"Okay, so why don't you want to marry her?" she asked.

"I do. I just don't want to hurt her. My life is real, ya hear me?" Saint said as his New Orleans drawl emerged in his dialect. He was good about hiding his strong New Orleans accent, but when he spoke from the heart, it always seemed to peek its head. He continued, "This life is not fit for marriage. I'm knee-deep in this shit. I want to wait until things slow down for me so that I can focus on her. But on the flip side, I can't make her wait forever. Does this make sense?" Saint said, seeking guidance. Pandora gently squeezed his hands and took a deep breath.

"You ever lie to her, you ever lied to this woman you speak of?" Pandora asked.

"Yeah, I have. Only to protect her feelings, though," he replied.

"She's found out about these lies that we speak of?" Pandora quizzed. Saint simply nodded his head, confirming her suspicions.

"Let me tell you something about a woman, and I need you to listen closely," Pandora spoke. She paused and turned her head to the side, staring at nothing in particular, searching for the correct words.

"Be careful about lying to your woman. Every time she forgives you, you will love her a little more. However, with your lies, she will begin to love you a little less. So, the day you love her the most will be the day that she will love you the least." Those words sent shivers throughout Saint's body, and the heaviness of his heart resonated deeply within his chest.

"Now, that advice is on the house. Something to grow on," Pandora stated as she released her grasp and focused back on the crystals that were on the table. She realigned her crystals, placing them correctly. Saint thought about her words, and just that quick, he made a decision. He decided if he beat his current case, he wouldn't waste any time in marrying his woman.

Saint smiled and placed the bricks on the table as Pandora began the baptism. As always, Saint just sat back and watched. The process never took too long, and some would say it was a waste of time, but ever since his connect suggested this, he had never been pinched by the law. Therefore, he never took his chances and skipped the process. He had a routine, and it had been that way for years. He would see his connect, and, on his way out, he would always stop by and see Pandora. Some would call it superstitious, but Saint called it playing the game the way it was supposed to be played. He listened as she chanted . . .

Afterward, Saint carefully placed the bricks back into his leather bag but not before sliding an envelope filled with cash over the table to Pandora. She smiled and received the money. Saint gathered himself and his bags, then stood up. He bent down and kissed Pandora on the cheek as he always did and then headed out.

As Saint reached the door, he turned back and found Pandora looking at him while smiling. He returned the smile and proceeded out. As he glanced at the wall just by the exit, he saw writing on the wall. The word "*Duality*" was written in what seemed to be a kid's handwriting. It stood out because it wasn't a common word that a child or someone of an adolescent age would write, and the word stuck with him. Saint never used the word before, so he was somewhat unfamiliar with the term.

"The more you live . . . the more you'll understand. I'll see you after dark for that other matter," Pandora said as if she were reading his mind as he tried to ponder about the meaning.

Saint said nothing and walked out. As he entered the hallway, the sound of the young girl's voice picked back up, getting louder with each step. She was singing the same lullaby as if she had never stopped singing. Saint noticed that the sound was slightly different than what he remembered. It now sounded like multiple voices were singing the song in unison. As he entered the main room, he saw the little girl sitting on the floor. However, this time, she seemed to be sitting across from another young child. They both had the same look, same gown, and same skin tones. The other child was a boy with a short haircut.

Twins? he thought as he walked past and eyed the two. With the girl, he could see her face fully, but the other child's back was turned to him as they playfully slapped hands while singing. Saint thought it was odd. He started to second-guess his memory, knowing that there was only one girl before. He shook his head and chalked it up as a mental lapse. As he walked toward the exit, he turned back to look at the children. All of a sudden, they stopped singing, and it grew eerily silent. The little girl that faced him smiled, showing her big blue eyes. Saint smiled back, and as the young boy slowly turned around, Saint held his smile, ready to greet him as well—but when he saw him, a wave of fear and confusion swept through his body.

What the fuck? Saint thought as the smile quickly faded from his face. The young boy had no facial features—nothing. No eyes, no mouth, nose, or eyebrows. Saint's mind spun rapidly, trying to make sense of what he was seeing. He looked at the girl, and she was smiling, like there was nothing unusual about her counterpart's deformity. The faceless little boy vaguely turned his head sideways, tilting his head to the side. This freaked Saint out as he shook his head in disbelief. He hurried out and wondered what the fuck he had just seen. Just as he reached the outside and felt the rays of the sun, he leaned against the house to catch his breath. Then, once more, he heard the kids sing. Saint looked down the block and noticed that it was now empty, a far cry from the happy, energetic scene from earlier. He took a deep breath, inhaling through his nose, and briefly closing his eyes to recenter himself.

Five little monkeys jumping on the bed
One fell off and bumped his head
Mama called the doctor, and the doctor said
No more . . . monkeys . . . jumping on the bed

Saint gripped his bag tightly and headed away from the house, but the sound of something crashing against the ground startled him, making him jump back. A monkey lay there as a maroon-colored puddle of blood seeped out of its body. Horrific-looking brain matter from the monkey's skull was splattered against the ground and instantly made Saint's stomach churn. He quickly looked away, not wanting to see the gruesome sight. It seemed as if the monkey had fallen from the building to its death. Saint looked up to see a lone monkey on the top of the roof dancing around while looking down at its dead companion.

Saint hurried away as he heard his phone ringing from his bag. He retrieved the phone and looked at the caller ID. It was his right-hand man, Zoo. His phone wasn't a usual one or even an up-to-date one, for that matter. His oversized Nokia phone had a long, rubber antenna sticking from it. It was at least fifteen years old and was totally outdated. Saint used this type of phone for many reasons, but the obvious one was its lack of technology. Older phones lacked the capabilities of being traced and were much more difficult to tap remotely. The long antenna allowed him to reach anywhere completely under the radar in North or South America. No phone towers were needed to correspond with the opposite party. It was basically a ramped-up walkie-talkie, and that's the device of choice he talked business on.

"Peace," Saint said, answering.

"Peace. We good?" Zoo asked.

"Absolutely. On my way back home now."

"God is good," Zoo said, smiling through the phone.

"Amen," Saint said, as he made his way down the block, where an antique car was waiting for him.

Saint pressed the *end* button and made his way to the end of the block. He saw the male driver just down the road. He was Cuban and stood no taller than five feet. The driver was waiting for Saint patiently as he leaned against the rear of the car with his arms folded. The man had olive-colored skin and wore a straw fedora hat. He seemed to be in his early 60s. Saint used him for transportation every time he visited the country, and he escorted him around in his 1960 Ford. The driver's name was Pedro.

The car was a faded red color, and you could tell that it had been sunburned over the years. The car didn't look like much on the outside. It had various rust spots, holes, and bald tires. It had been through many harsh days, and its war wounds proved it. Nevertheless, it ran like a horse, and that's all Saint could really ask for.

As Saint got closer, the man said something in Spanish and opened the rear door, giving Saint a clear path to slide in. Saint slid in and threw his head back in the car seat, thinking about the peculiar day that he had. Something was different about today, and it gave him an eerie feeling deep within his soul.

As they cruised the Cuban roads doing fifteen miles per hour, it gave Saint time to reflect. He watched as kids chased the car and knocked on the windows. He would pass out money usually, but today was different. He kept seeing the boy's blank, deformed face. He wanted to blame it on stress, but he knew better. Something was happening. He just couldn't put his finger on it. He prided himself on having a sharp mind, but this was an occurrence that he could not wrap his thoughts around. His brain was playing tricks on him in the worst way.

Or was it?

He thought about the words of Pandora and the day's events. He looked to his left and saw the bag that would be distributed throughout the bayou, making him a quick seven figures when it was done. He wanted out, and the main reason for that was so that he could become the man that the love of his life deserved. With what he saw this day, he knew someone or "something" was trying to tell him something. He just didn't know what exactly.

A beautiful cathedral church was the setting for the day's special event. Luxury cars lined the parking lot of the historic church. It was a gathering of bosses, family, and well-respected figures throughout the bayou. Stunning, hand-crafted statues of angels peppered the marbled floors, and tall podiums were the pillars of the immaculate haven. Three months had passed, and Saint was at a major crossroads in his life. He stared at himself in the full-length mirror and straightened up his bow tie, examining it very carefully. His shiny, bald head and huge, shaped beard were flawless. His well-tailored Tom Ford suit was all white, and the Italian cut fit him impeccably. His belly had even shrunk a size or two. He hung the expensive suit very well. He looked like he stepped straight out of a *GQ* magazine.

Today was the big day. He was marrying the woman who held the key to his heart, Ramina. The room had five other men inside, all of them talking amongst each other, sipping Cognac, and prepping for their leader's new union. They all were suited as well and accented with traditional black accessories. Saint was in the presence of his groomsmen, his team. Although none of them shared the same bloodline, they were family by way of the drug game.

Saint was a boss. He was the natural leader and the sole connect to the Cuban heroin plug. Although Saint was younger than some of his men, he held the most wisdom. He moved as if he were twenty years older than his actual age. He never did anything fast. His speech, his movements, his business moves were always slow and well calculated. Saint never spoke loudly. No one ever heard him raise his voice. He did everything on his own terms and in his own tone. He controlled "the board" at all times. Saint was the man that made the operation go. He was at the top of the totem pole, and it was the best-kept secret in the bayou.

Zoo approached Saint and straightened up his tie. He then threw his arm around Saint's shoulder and leaned in to talk to him. Zoo hugged him tightly.

"Today is the day, bruh. You finally about to do it," Zoo said proudly.

Saint nodded in agreement without saying a word. He looked at Zoo through the mirror and faintly smirked at his best friend. Zoo stood about six foot and had a slim build. His skin complexion was as dark as night—so dark that he almost looked purple. He wore a neatly cut Caesar hairstyle and 360 waves wrapped around his head flawlessly. He wore Cartier frames with wood grain around the rim of the glasses. He was from Flint, Michigan, and it was very prevalent in his style. He migrated to Nola ten years before, when he went to school at Louisiana Tech on an athletic scholarship. He ended up staying after his college stint and began his new career in the drug trade. In his newfound game is where he met Saint, and they had been tight ever since. He served as the underboss to Saint and was the buffer between Saint and the rest of the wolves that the job came with. Saint was more behind-the-scenes, and he moved ghostlike.

An old saying was "if you know, you know," and this term explained Saint's entire being to the fullest. He was a quiet storm in the drug game, and not everyone knew who he was, but all the *right* people knew who he was. Saint was what you called a "street king," and, on that day, the king would finally be getting his queen.

"Mina is getting a good nigga," Zoo said, having a heart-to-heart with his partner in crime. Saint slyly slid his hands in his slacks and walked over to the window that was facing the beautiful acreage behind the church. Without even looking around the room, Saint spoke.

"Give Zoo and me a minute alone," he said in his low, deep baritone. He didn't speak loudly, but when he spoke . . . people listened. Therefore, the room cleared out immediately, and Saint waited patiently as the men exited the room. Saint casually glanced back and made sure everyone was gone and only he and Zoo occupied the room before he spoke.

After the last groomsman left and the door was closed, Saint spoke. "Zoo, I'm done," he said with conviction and without a doubt. Zoo grew a look of concern on his face and walked over to Saint, joining him by the window.

"What?" Zoo asked, not believing what he was hearing.

"I'm out. I'm flying straight. I'm done with the game," Saint said.

"Wait . . . We are just getting started. How can you pull the plug? Listen, I know you on your married man shit, but we still out here in the trenches. We ain't ready to hang it up just yet. We got the entire bayou sewn up. We can't just shut down shop like that," Zoo pleaded as he was now standing in front of Saint.

"Don't worry. I'm giving you the plug. I'm done with it. It's yours now," Saint answered.

"Don't play, bro . . ." Zoo said as a wave of excitement overcame him. He shot a look of optimism in the direction of Saint and tried to read him. Throughout the years, Saint had never introduced Zoo to his Cuban plug. He always kept them separate and went alone. However, he was at a place in his life where he had enough money to retire comfortably, and he did not need the game. He was 34 years old and was ready to build a legit life with his new wife.

"Nah, I'm serious. After I get back from the honeymoon, I'm going to introduce you to the Cuban connect. It's yours now. The whole operation is yours now. I'm out," Saint said, reconfirming his exit.

Zoo couldn't hold in his emotions. He hugged Saint so tightly and firmly, understanding that Saint had just changed his life forever. With a plug like that, the sky was the limit, and it was something that any dope boy dreamed of. Zoo nearly had tears in his eyes as he released his embrace and looked at his best friend. Unlike Saint, Zoo had no escape plan for the game. He loved everything about it. All he wanted to be was a kingpin, and he was willing to take anything that came with it. In his mind, the reward of being the number one guy outweighed the pitfalls that accompanied the position. He was eating good under Saint, but he didn't have the power or the respect of Saint. And *that's* what he yearned for.

“I won’t let you down, bruh. That’s my word,” Zoo said with belief.

As always, Saint acted as if someone were listening, so he spoke low as he leaned forward and put his lips near Zoo’s right earlobe.

“We’ll fly out to Cuba, and I’ll personally introduce you to Alejandro,” he whispered, referring to the connect. He gently tapped Zoo’s cheek and continued. “Take this mu’fucka over,” He then reached over and grabbed the champagne bottle that was sitting in the bucket of ice. Zoo grabbed a champagne flute, and the sound of the cork being popped echoed throughout the room. They both shared a toast as the sound of the bell rang throughout the church, which was his signal. It was time for the ceremony to start.

“Yo, quick thing. I was going to wait, but I want to get on top of this while you’re away on your honeymoon. We ran into a little problem,” Zoo said as he reached into the inside pocket of his blazer. He pulled out a small Baggie. Saint’s eyes went directly to it, and he noticed the stamp on the front. It had a US seal on it with words underneath it. It simply read “*Cubana.*” It caught Saint’s attention because that was his signature stamp that he put on his heroin. However, he could tell that it wasn’t his because the logo was slightly off. He knew from the jump that it was a copycat.

“You know how the game go, beloved. Niggas gon’ imitate. Don’t trip on that,” Saint said calmly as he grabbed the pack and studied it.

“True, but this shit killing niggas. Four people overdosed this month off this pack. The mix ain’t right, man. Somebody putting some shit in the game.”

“You take it to Jeremy?” Saint asked, referring to their lab technician that they had on payroll.

“Yeah, he said it’s bogus. It’s laced with acetyl fentanyl,” Zoo responded while shaking his head.

"What's that?" Saint asked as he slightly frowned.

"Fake dope. Synthetic," said Zoo.

"Who putting this out with our stamp on it?" Saint questioned as his brows frowned.

"That's the million-dollar question, my guy. We don't know. But this shit is flooded all through the bayou."

"And you say how many people overdosed off this bullshit?" Saint said as he shook the bag in front of Zoo's face.

"Four as of last night. Plus, you know the heat that bodies bring. We don't need that type of attention," Zoo answered.

Saint instantly became concerned, and his mind put a plan together. He held the Baggie up to the light with one hand and flicked it with his index finger.

"You have to get to the bottom of this. I told you what time I'm on. I'm dead serious, beloved. This isn't my concern anymore."

"I know, I know. But you know how I get down. I'm about to start shaking shit up until I get some answers," Zoo stated. Saint knew exactly what Zoo was referring to when he said, "shaking shit up," and Saint didn't want to take the leash off Zoo. Zoo was a hothead, and Saint didn't want to exchange the hands of power while in the middle of bloodshed. He knew he would have to get to the bottom of it before he completely walked away. He wanted his exit to be smooth and quiet—not like this.

Just as Saint was about to respond, the door swung open, and a petite woman that looked to be in her late fifties came in. She had a small gray Afro, and her face was made up. She wore an evening gown that matched the accent color of the wedding. Saint swiftly placed the pack of dope inside his pocket to hide it. It was his mother.

"Hey, Ma," Saint said, hoping she didn't see what he was just holding up. He especially didn't want her to see it because of her past addiction. She had been clean for only about ten years.

"Hey, baby," she said while smiling from ear to ear. Her bright smile was on full display as she waved her son over. "Come on, now. The pastor is ready for you. It's almost time to start."

"Yes, ma'am," Saint said respectfully as he nodded his head. He watched as his mom waited for him and waved him over hastily.

"We'll talk about this later, beloved," Saint whispered to Zoo. Zoo nodded in agreement, and they both headed toward the exit and prepared to go to the main chapel.

A small-framed woman stood before the cathedral's steps as she looked up at the historic place of worship. Her green eyes and caramel skin tone made her unique, and her tattooed body only added to that. She had a small tattooed heart under her left eye that was the lone marking on her flawless face. Various tattoos covered her neck, body, and even her fingers. Over thirty-five tattoos covered her entire body, which only added flair to her distinctiveness. She had a ruggedness about herself, yet was still feminine. Her Cuban descent shined through her features, so there was no hiding her heritage. Her smoky-brown skin resembled that of the people of her native land.

Tay tried her best to tame her frazzled hair as she repeatedly rubbed it down. What once was a silky-smooth mane was now brittle, wild, and all over her head. Her tattooed hands were ashy and in need of moisturizing. A wave of embarrassment overcame her as she looked up at the beautiful church before her and then down at her attire. She wore a soiled, tight-fitting jogging suit with a small jean jacket over it. She hadn't changed clothes for a week straight. She knew that she hadn't bathed in a while and probably smelled just like she felt. Nevertheless, something seemed to pull her to that place, on that day. She had to see Saint one last time before he started his new life.

Tay had heard through the grapevine that this wedding was more than just a nuptial, but it served as his retirement party to the game. The streets were speaking, and it was a day that the bayou shut down to honor its Most Valuable Player. She heard the sound of the bells ringing and instantly felt sick to her stomach. She abruptly bent over and threw up on the church steps, dry heaving as she gripped her abdomen. She was nervous and heartbroken at the same time. She was there to see the man she was in love with marry someone else. She wanted to be happy for him, but her somewhat selfish heart wouldn't allow that to happen.

Thoughts invaded her mind, asking God why he wasn't marrying her. After all that she had been through in life, it seemed like she deserved him more. The pain of meeting her soul mate, knowing that he could never be hers, was a pain that she could never have fathomed. Most people think physical pain is the worst thing in life, but try living with regret. That is true pain because there was no real end to that feeling. Regret is everlasting. It will eat you alive quicker than any cancer known to man. She knew that she had kept things away from Saint that would make him look at her differently. Therefore, she realized that she did not deserve him. The agony of knowing that was a pain that she knew would never fade away. *Too many secrets,* she thought to herself.

She gathered herself, stood straight up as she wiped her mouth, and then took a deep breath. Slowly, she walked up the stairs and then through the humongous French-style opening. She pulled the heavy doors, parting them, and walked in. The scene was breathtaking. It was something that she would only read about in fairy tales, and she was blown away. She could hear the distinct sound of the cello playing and the chatter from the guests that occupied the chapel. As she made her way toward it, she heard the sound of footsteps echoing throughout the lobby. She turned back and saw a man walking her way. He was barely paying attention to her as he made his way toward the chapel as well. As the man got closer, she saw and instantly noticed that it was one of Saint's henchmen, Gunner. She tried to bow her head to avoid eye contact, but the man had already made out who she was.

"Tay?" Gunner said as he squinted his eyes, trying to see if it was her. The young man used to have a crush on Tay, so seeing her like that instantly saddened him.

"Hey," she said shamefully as she tried to fix her hair. She slid the hair that was over her face behind her ear and folded her arms in front of her chest.

"Damn, I haven't seen you around in a while," he said nervously as he couldn't bring himself to make eye contact with the girl that he had lusted over once before.

"I know, right?" Tay said with a forced, nervous smile. Her eyes were wavering and unsteady. She, as well, couldn't bring herself to look at the young man in the eyes. She was in the middle of a drug binge and knew that it was showing through her appearance.

He couldn't believe how bad she looked. He felt a sense of pity for her. He was embarrassed for her. He could smell the absence of cleanliness bouncing off of her and dropped his head in disbelief.

The young man looked over his shoulders to see if anyone was looking at them. Then he shook his head and focused back on Tay. "Look, you shouldn't have come here. You know that," he admitted, not wanting her to mess up his boss's big day. Everyone in the hood knew what had happened the time she was around, and she was the last person that he thought would be at the wedding.

"I know, I know. I just wanted to say congratulations. I shouldn't have come," Tay admitted, and as she brushed past him and stormed toward the exit, Gunner grabbed her by the arm, stopping her.

"Hey . . . hey. Look, take this," he said under his breath as he took his free hand and reached down into his pants pocket. He pulled out a wad of money and quickly slid a hundred-dollar bill off his rubber-banded roll. He held it up in front of Tay, between his pointer and index fingers.

Tay's eyes shot to the money, and her mind instantly started to race. She thought about the drugs she could buy with that and shoot directly into her veins for the high that she had been chasing after that entire morning. Her heart pounded, and an insatiable urge overtook her. Her hand involuntarily went to the back of her neck to tame the sudden itch that overcame her. She immediately became fidgety. She looked like a full-blown fiend, and the young hustler instantly felt terrible for her. She was his age, and to see her tweak like that was heartbreaking. It was like he could see her thought processes. It was evident that she was trying to fight the urge to take the money as she stared at it intensely. She was twitching and scratching at the same time, which was making it uncomfortable for him to watch. She was at her rock bottom, and it was apparent.

"Just take it," he whispered in a pleading voice, knowing that she needed a fix so she wouldn't get any sicker than she already was. He was a dealer of heroin, so he knew the internal battle she was going through. That same feeling that was killing her was the same one that kept him in business and paid. His only worry was that word would get back to Saint that he gave Tay money so that she could get high. However, he felt sorry for her. He just wanted to help.

Just as he was about to say something else, the doors opened, and the sunlight shined into the lobby. It was the bride coming with a group of other women through the front doors, and she was headed in their direction. It was time for the wedding.

Tay focused on the woman in the big, flowing dress. The dress was glamorous and elegant. The sheer, tube-like dress was tight fitting but opened beautifully the closer it got to the ground. She looked like an ebony mermaid. Her train dragged at least eight feet behind her, and a stylist followed her and held up the rear of the gown. Tay's heart dropped when she saw how beautiful she was. She wished deep down in her heart that she was in that beautiful dress rather than Ramina. Tears welled up in her eyes, and her bottom lip quivered. Pain filled her chest, and she felt anxious. Her breath became short, and a flutter in her heart made her feel like she was about to die right there on the marble floor. She had never felt that feeling before. She placed her hand on her chest, and it seemed like the only thing she could hear was the sound of her own breathing. It was as if the world had slowed down, and Ramina was walking in slow motion toward them. She stared at Ramina's beautiful made-up face and deep maroon lipstick and was in awe. She was absolutely beautiful.

"Come on," the young man said as he wrapped his arm around Tay. He then guided her toward the sanctuary, not wanting her to ruin the wedding. Ramina was so busy gathering herself and talking amongst her squad that she didn't even notice Tay by the chapel door. Tay and Gunner took a seat in the last row, slipping in unnoticed.

Tay glanced at the head of the church. Her eyes frantically searched for Saint, trying to locate the only man she truly ever loved. She was eager to see him. It had been almost a year since she had been in his presence, and her anxiety skyrocketed. The way that man made her feel was second to none, and no drug could compare to the high that Saint was capable of giving her. She was captivated by him and his aura. Saint was a vibe. A vibe that she couldn't get anywhere else on planet Earth. He was always calm . . . always slow motion. His voice was like violins in her mind because it never got loud or off-key. His voice soothed her. Her heart raced, just thinking about his baritone. Saint was that nigga, second to none. The most impressive trait he had was the fact that he didn't even know it. And if he did, he didn't show it. His humble demeanor made him even more appealing. She smiled, seeing him in the crisp suit. She caught a glimpse of his pearly white teeth as he and Zoo talked with each other.

"He's so handsome," she whispered as a tear involuntarily slipped down her face. She quickly wiped it away and sniffled. Although she was sad, she was happy for him because he seemed to be joyful. The look on his face told his story. He seemed as if he were content, and that was true. He had finally found peace in his life. Saint was about to exit at the top of the game, and that day served as a retirement party as well as a wedding. Tay saw the line of groomsmen and bridesmaids at the helm of the place and watched closely as Zoo and Saint smiled and whispered to each other while standing there waiting for the bride to enter. The loud sounds of the organ played, and everyone immediately stood. Everyone except Tay, that is. She sat there with her hands on her lap as the sea of guests stood up around her.

Everyone's eyes shot to the entrance and waited patiently for the woman of the hour. The sounds of the wedding song were like a dagger to her heart as she closed her eyes. Every note tugged at Tay's heart, and she thought that she would have a heart attack right then and there during the ceremony in front of everyone.

Suddenly, the large church doors swung open, revealing the bride to be. By now, the tears flowed nonstop as she started to hear the gasps and chatter. Tay chanted something incoherently under her breath as the woman made her way down the aisle. She mumbled nothings in a low tone as the tears continued to flow. She watched Ramina walk past her with her beautiful white dress. A glamorous, sheer veil was over her face, but it didn't hide it well. Her watering eyes and pretty smile were on full display as she slowly made her way to her soon-to-be husband.

Tay watched as the man that she loved waited for the woman at the end of the aisle . . . that was not her. She couldn't take the pressure and quickly slipped out the back door once the bride made it to the front of the church.

Chapter One

A Toast to the Assholes

The sound of yet another plate being dropped by the waiters erupted. The shattering sound had become a part of the party, it seemed like. That was the third plate broken during the reception. People paused for a second to look over at the mishap but continued to finish up their meals as they ate the 5-star New Orleans cuisine, compliments of the chef hired by Saint and Ramina.

"You peep what's going on, bruh?" Zoo whispered as he leaned over toward Saint as they sat at the head table. Saint listened closely and then scanned the almost full reception hall. He vaguely grinned and calmly nodded his head in agreement. Saint always chose gestures over words if he could, picking and choosing when he spoke.

"That's exactly what I thought too. I knew I wasn't tripping," Zoo said as he sat back upright and fixed his blazer and adjusted his Cartier frames. He took a sip of champagne directly from the bottle and scanned the room. Champagne was flowing, and the reception was in full swing. It had been a few hours since the wedding, and now it was time for the celebration.

The vibe was a positive one, and the sounds of smooth R&B played in the background, acting as a soundtrack for the night. The reception was only for a selected few, and it was the ending of a great night. Only Saint's closest friends, business associates, and the waitstaff were in attendance. No extras. Although the crowd was small, there was a lot of power present in the building. Saint had earned a lot of respect throughout the years. Therefore, his guest list was one of importance. A few of the soldiers from Saint's blocks were there, but the guest list was mostly criminals. It was a den of hustlers and urban legends. At least a dozen street millionaires attended, all of whom Saint supplied, making that possible.

His wedding was a meeting of the elites. Everyone who was somebody came out to pay respect to Saint. Saint got just as many farewells as he did congratulations. He was moving away from the bayou and heading away for good, and everyone that ate with him knew this. Saint was the plug and the source of many men's life aspirations. He and Ramina would ride off into the sunset, leaving the life that had afforded him his luxurious lifestyle. Saint had sucked the streets dry and saved up enough money to retire comfortably from the life. He set out a plan, and he was at its pinnacle. His exit plan was well calculated. After his honeymoon, he and Ramina would retire in Miami.

A long table stood at the head of the room, and the groomsmen and bridesmaids all accompanied the newlyweds. Food had been served, and it was time for the best man to give a speech, honoring his right-hand man. Zoo stood up and grabbed a butter knife and tapped it against the wineglass, causing a chime to sound throughout the place. Everyone stopped moving and talking. Heads turned, and all their focus was now on Zoo. The DJ lowered the music that was playing throughout the speakers, and just like that, the entire place was quiet. The only people that were moving were the waiters who were picking up the dirty dishes from the different tables throughout the room. Zoo spoke loudly so everyone could hear him.

“My name is Zoey. My friends call me Zoo, if y’all didn’t already know.”

“Zoooo!” someone yelled from the crowd causing Zoo to pause briefly and then look in their direction. He smiled.

“See this nigga to my left? That’s my guy right there. The best friend I’ve ever had. Not a man of a lot of words, but when he speaks . . . he speaks of substance. When he speaks, it means power. See, Saint and I met years ago when I was a senior in college. I had just blown out my knee and didn’t know what I was going to do in life. He showed me a new way of thinking. He showed me that I didn’t need a lot of friends, just one good one. And I found that in him. My mu’fuckin’ partner in crime. We got a lot of money together too. We started a real estate company and haven’t looked back since,” Zoo said and hesitated as he shot a look over to Saint and winked. Saint smiled, knowing that they hadn’t sold one damn house together a day of their lives. Honestly, that was the first time he ever heard something about a real estate company. Saint shook his head in amusement as he tapped Ramina’s leg under the table. She chuckled as well, catching on to the inside joke.

“Zoo crazy as hell,” Ramina playfully murmured under her breath. She whispered so low that only Saint could hear her. Saint picked up his glass and saluted Zoo, followed by a simple nod. Zoo continued.

“Saint always did right by me and showed me what real friendship is. I tell you all the time, there’s not a lot of people that’s cut from our cloth. Not too many niggas like us. He told me once that when it comes to friends . . . less is more, so there’s plenty of us.” Random encouraging shouts from the crowd came from the guests as Zoo’s words resonated with them. He was preaching a ghetto sermon.

"I know that's right!" a lady yelled as she clapped her hands.

"Talk to 'em!" another man yelled as if Zoo were in a pulpit.

Zoo paused a moment and picked up his champagne flute. He raised the glass in the air and looked as the waiters continued to do their jobs, not paying him any attention. Then he picked up his speech right where he left off. "I want to wish him and his beautiful wife, Ramina, the best, as they start this new chapter in their lives. I love you both from the bottom of my heart," Zoo said as he dropped his head, signaling that he was done. But he quickly scanned the room and said something in addition.

"And another thing . . . I want to thank the waitstaff for the phenomenal job they're doing tonight. Let's give 'em a round of applause," he said as he motioned for people to clap. The crowd clapped, and a few of the waiters smiled but didn't pay too much attention. They were staying on the task at hand.

"Now, I want everyone to do one more thing for me. Raise your fist like this," Zoo said as he put his fist in the air. People were confused about what exactly he was doing. However, slowly but surely, the guests raised their fists. Zoo looked back at Saint to see if his hand was raised.

Saint just smiled and shook his head. Saint knew that his friend was a charismatic character and sat back and watched the show, not wanting any part of what was about to happen. Once Zoo saw all the hands in the air, he finished off his speech.

"Now stick up your finger like so," he said, as he waved his middle finger in the air. "All these waiters are federal agents, trying to find something out . . . but they won't. We are all law-abiding citizens in this mu'fucka. So, this is a toast to y'all bitch-ass mu'fuckas. Nice try. Spend these good folks' tax money on something that makes a difference," Zoo said with a big smile on his face. The entire room had their middle fingers in the air, and all the attention went on the mostly male waitstaff.

The waiters paused, and their pale white faces all blushed red. There was no denying what Zoo had said. It was the truth. One of the male waiters seemed to be so irate that he couldn't hide it any longer. The 40-something-year-old Caucasian man stood there in shock. He clenched his jaws tightly, and his pale white skin instantaneously turned plum red. It looked like smoke was about to pour out of his ears, he was so hot. Out of pure frustration, he dropped the handful of plates he carried and stormed off. Their cover had been blown, and it seemed almost instantly the other waiters followed suit. The sounds of glasses shattering erupted because multiple "waiters" dropped their plates and walked out. The guests, still with their middle fingers in the air, laughed uncontrollably. They literally laughed the Feds out of the building. It was a beautiful moment.

They say that the Feds have a 98 percent success rate, but on that night, they lost to the streets. It was a historic moment for the bad guys. Saint couldn't do anything but laugh as he shook his head at Zoo. Saint had known about the setup for a little over a month, and rather than complain, he let it play out. The Feds were always trying to find something on him but never could. The recent murder case that he had thrown out made them put him under a microscope. The careful and strategic measures that Saint took to protect himself over the years had all paid off. No paper trail connected him to his empire, and the only blemish he had on his jacket was the murder, and that wasn't even drug related. That incident was personal. He watched as Zoo walked back over to him and took a seat next to him. The DJ played the music again, and everyone talked among themselves at the crazy turn of events. It only added to the legend of Saint. That night was one for the record books.

It was just a few ticks after midnight, and most of the guests were beginning to exit. However, Saint and his wife were still there, enjoying the moment and dancing the night away. They must have had the DJ spin back Lauryn Hill's "Nothing Even Matters" about ten times. The two swayed back and forth as Ramina sang their favorite parts of the song in his ear while snapping her fingers to the snares. Saint's hand was on the small of her back, and her arms hung from his neck as they slowly rocked in perfect unison together. Saint's bow tie was untied, and the first two buttons on his shirt were unbuttoned. He was feeling good as he looked into the eyes of his new wife. Ramina was tipsy, and both of their hearts were full of joy as the thought of their new life had both of them in a blissful, trance-like state. He held a large bottle of champagne in his free hand and smiled at Ramina while gazing deeply into her soul's windows.

"Mi, you're beautiful. You're perfect," he complimented in admiration. He called her "Mi" for short, and she loved it every time she heard it. Her thick frame and wide hips made Saint's mind think about what they were going to do after they left. He looked at her face and admired her skin tone. Her full lips and made-up face were that of perfection like a ghetto Barbie. Baby hairs rested on her edges as her hair lay perfectly. He slid his hand down to her plump backside and cupped her ass, giving it a slight squeeze.

"You always know what to say to make me smile, Saint," Ramina said as she gazed into her husband's slightly red eyes. It made her smile, knowing that he was happy and finally letting loose for a night. He seldom drank, so he was in rare form.

"It's my truth, love. I'm just speaking about what I see. You're the prettiest girl in the world to me. You been here since the beginning, and I appreciate everything. I appreciate your loyalty. For that, I owe you the world," Saint said with sincerity, never breaking eye contact with his lady.

"You're my soul mate, Saint Von Cole," she said as she smiled and looked at her man in admiration.

"You're my soul mate, Ramina Shay Cole," he said, playfully returning the sentiment. They both shared a small laugh and continued to rock.

"Can I ask you a question, mister?" she said.

"Of course, love. Ask me anything," he answered.

"Are you going to leave it alone? Are you done? Like, done-done?"

"Of course," Saint said, as he looked around. "I'm out. There's nothing left for me to do in that world. I'm out," Saint confirmed. He spoke with conviction and was confident in his decision. He was out of the game for good. He saw the skepticism in her face, although she remained silent and nodded her head in contentment. Saint knew that, like everyone else, it was hard to believe.

"I can stay and die, or I can bow out gracefully and live the rest of my life with my best friend. Seems like an easy choice, you hear me?" Saint explained charmingly. He ran his tongue across his top row of teeth and smiled. It was contagious because it instantly made Ramina beam.

She shook her head, blushing.

"What?" Saint asked, wanting to know why she was smiling.

"You always make things so easy. Everything is so easy with you. You never cease to amaze me. You always have an answer to a situation."

Saint pulled her close to his chest and gently kissed her on her forehead. He whispered that he loved her and inhaled deeply as she lay her head on his chest, vibing to the rhythm of the beat and his soul at the same time.

Saint knew that a wise man knows how to make something complicated seem simple. Yet, a fool takes something simple and makes it complicated. Saint understood this, so he moved accordingly. Little did she know, he had been planning his exit for years. Everything that was happening now was a direct result of his strategic thinking. He would always think about a situation in ten different ways before he even told a soul about it, and this instance was no different.

As the song wrapped up, three girls dressed in bridesmaids' gowns approached the newlyweds. The song switched to what the locals called "Bounce" music. Bounce music was legendary in the bayou. The upbeat, fast tempo style was a staple in the culture of New Orleans, and it wasn't a party officially until you had the bounce. The sounds of Big Freedia pumped out of the speakers, and Ramina and her girls all come together while forming a small circle. Saint stepped to the side and smiled, watching his wife have a good time with her girls. That's when he felt the arm of Zoo wrap around him.

"You did it, my nigga," he said just before taking a big gulp from the champagne bottle.

"It feels right," Saint replied as the two stepped off the dance floor, walking side by side.

"Can you believe the fuzz came in this mu'fucka on your wedding day? They will stoop to the lowest of lows to lock a nigga up, won't they?" Zoo said, shaking his head, still in disbelief.

"They can snoop all they want. They ain't got shit on me. Let 'em come. I'm not worried at all," Saint said confidently.

"No doubt . . . No doubt," Zoo replied. He watched as the girls enjoyed themselves and yelled loudly while gyrating their backsides. He loved Ramina's crew because they were all beautiful, young, and rich. They were a power circle, and each one of them had a nice hustle going on. They were infamous throughout the city for being bad girls that loved the bad boys. Ramina was the ringleader of their crew, for sure. She complemented Saint very well by owning one of the most prominent salons in the city, and her online hair store did seven figures each year. Ramina wasn't your typical dope man's wife. She had her own, which made her even more desirable.

Zoo watched closely as the girls moved their big asses in circles in unison and eyed the one he would proposition later. But first, he wanted to talk business with Saint. Saint could turn someone from a small-time hustler into a king with the snap of a finger. Saint was the source of every drug dealer's happiness. He could change their lives with one simple phone call.

"About what you said earlier, I really appreciate that. I been waiting to take my shit to the next level. This is my way to do that," Zoo explained.

"Indeed. Indeed," Saint simply replied.

"I'm expanding," Zoo said, as he stared at nothing in particular. Saint could tell that he was planning his next move. The ambition was pouring out of him. Saint knew that was his best trait, but it also could be his worst.

"Expanding, huh?" Saint said.

"Yeah, I'm going to shoot back home and set up shop in Flint. I have a few cats out there that's moving around. They just need a steady pipeline to feed their people, feel me?" Zoo explained.

"After I get back from the honeymoon, we are on the first thing smoking to Cuba," Saint assured him.

"Cubana," Zoo said as he did a bad interpretation of a Spanish accent. He continued, "Oh yeah, I need you to plug me with homegirl too. You know . . . your witch doctor out there. I need that shit on my side, just in case shit goes left. I still can't believe that case got dropped. No trial—not nothing. Whatever you paid that woman . . . It was worth it."

"Was it worth it?" Saint asked. He was asking himself that question, more so than Zoo. "And she's not a witch doctor," Saint said as he shook his head at his friend's misconception. "It's not that simple. There's more to it than just voodoo dolls and that bullshit you see in movies," Saint said, as he had mental flashes of the things he saw on his last trip. He had been there plenty of times before, but that last time, things were definitely different.

Chapter Two

Monkey on the Back

Bums and dope fiends were scattered in various huddles under the overpass. It was in the wee hours of the night when only the street zombies and hustlers were up with their own personal agendas. A congregation spot for the city's have-nots, homeless, and druggies was under the city bridge. Two different bonfires inside old aluminum trash cans were ablaze, also known as a poor man's heating system. As the small fires illuminated the dark area, bums circled them, waving their hands over the flames in an attempt to keep warm. The scene resembled Hades with how fires danced in the air, and soulless addicts wandered aimlessly. Some of them looked like statues that leaned to the side from the effects of the heroin's potency.

Tay had become a familiar face on the scene over the past few months. She was by far the youngest fiend on the scene. Earlier, she had left the church, which was only a block away. She slumped on the soiled sofa as she could barely keep her eyes open. She dazedly moaned as she tried to sit upright but flopped back because her upper torso felt as if it weighed a ton. She immediately melted back into the couch after her failed attempt.

She felt wetness in between her thighs and looked down to see a huge wet spot in her crotch area. She groggily woke up completely from her heroin-induced nod and realized that she had pissed herself. This was a common thing among junkies. The rush that an addict felt when the drugs traveled through their veins was described as orgasmic. The sensation was like no other and sometimes caused the urge to relieve yourself. Tay had taken the money that Gunner had given her at the wedding and went straight to the dope man for her fix. Before that day, she had been clean for an entire week. However, seeing Ramina walk down the aisle to Saint pushed her to try to numb the pain. She just wanted the pain in her heart to go away, and the only way she knew to do that was to get high.

She gathered herself and stood up. She straightened her jacket and rubbed her frazzled hair. She looked around and noticed the familiar faces under the bridge and felt a sharp pain shoot through her stomach. She doubled over in pain and vomited onto the pavement. She knew her body was about to become dope sick. She was on a countdown to being in unbearable pain if she didn't get another shot of dope in her veins. The small fix that she had gotten earlier wasn't enough to keep her from going through the motions of being ill.

Her eyes scanned her surroundings, then focused on the gas station across the street. She headed that way to see if she could catch a young hustler to try to make a trade. "A trade" was a term in the streets when fiends would trade sexual favors for drugs, and Tay was open to it all. She would do anything to get the monkey off her back and prevent herself from getting sick.

She made her way across the street, where two guys stood outside of the station with hoodies on. She crossed her arms and hugged herself tightly as she made her way over to them.

***

Saint opened the door to his black Range Rover and watched as his newly wedded wife stepped in. They were just outside of the reception hall that was near the church where they were just married. As he took a swallow of the champagne that was in his hand, he studied his wife closely, admiring her. He gulped the bottle and wiped his mouth as he swallowed. He then walked around the car and hopped into the driver's seat, but not before pulling off his blazer and placing it across the middle armrest. A packet of bad dope fell from his pocket and onto Ramina's lap. Ramina wasn't green to the game, so she immediately knew what it was. She picked it up and examined it.

"This looks different. This isn't Cubana," she said confidently as she examined the altered stamp.

"I know, I know. It's some fake shit going around, and I have to get to the bottom of it," Saint said as he placed his hand on the steering wheel.

"I thought you were out, Saint," Ramina said as a brief wave of disappointment was written all over her face.

"I know, love. I just want to get to the bottom of it before Zoo starts shooting up shit. You know how he is," Saint expounded.

"Yea, I know, but that's not your concern anymore. You promised that this was over, babe. You promised," Ramina pleaded.

"You know what? You're right," Saint admitted, knowing that if he didn't just walk away from the game, something would always pull him back in. Instantly, Ramina smiled like a young schoolgirl.

"Well, I'll get rid of this for you. I'm going to make sure you leave this shit alone. We are about to start our new life together. We're leaving the bayou for good. So it can just be us two," she said joyfully. She tucked the pack in her purse to ensure that Saint wouldn't follow up on the street issue.

He watched as Ramina immediately took off her Louboutin stiletto heels and rested her feet on the white carpet of his car. They caught each other's eyes and smiled, both thinking the same thing. They couldn't wait to reach their home so they could make love for the first time as husband and wife. The sexual tension had been building up all night, and they were lusting after each other. He watched as Ramina giggled and worked her dress up, exposing her bald vagina. She pressed her back against her door so that she was completely facing him. She put one of her legs on the dash so that he could get a perfect view of her love box. Her big, brown legs always turned Saint on as he smirked at her voluptuous physique. She spread her legs apart as far as she could and rested her head on the window. Saint slowly pulled off.

He looked over in awe and smiled as he watched as she gave him a show. She sexily put her fingers in her mouth and made sure that she put enough saliva on them to do the job. She then circled her tongue around her own fingers, dropping them down to her box.

"Oooh," she purred. The moment her wet fingers reached her clitoris, it pulsated. Ramina smiled in pleasure as she felt the heartbeat in her love box. She tenderly tapped her vagina, causing a loud, wet sound to erupt. With every tap, it seemed as if her button grew and grew, slightly peeking from her lips. She continued to moan, all while keeping eye contact with Saint. She then applied pressure to herself and slowly stroke herself in slow, circular motions. Saint tried his best to focus on the road, but it was hard to stay on track. His eyes went back and forth from the road to his girl. He felt his manhood begin to grow. He thought about how he would bend her over as soon as they walked through their door. Ramina took her foot and placed it on Saint's crotch, searching for his growing tool. Her foot stopped when she found it, and that's when her mouth watered.

"Yeah, I'm livin' like that," Saint said playfully in a deep New Orleans accent, showing off his girth and strength. His bottom row of golds was on full display as he ran his tongue across his white top row. She wanted to taste him and took it as a personal challenge to make him erupt before they reached home. She got on her knees, in the seat, and unbuckled his belt buckle. She frantically searched for his rod, and when she found it, she let out a satisfying moan. Saint leaned back his seat slightly while keeping one hand on the steering wheel. He lifted his shirt so he could get a clear view of what was about to happen. He watched as Ramina wrapped her full lips around him, slowly swirling her tongue around his tip before swallowing him whole. She slowly made him disappear and reappear, working her magic. The slurping sounds made the experience even more enticing for Saint as he let out an unintentional moan. She wiggled her ass in the air as she pleased him, and the sight made Saint even stronger.

As Ramina pleased him, a bell sounded. Saint's eyes drifted to the speedometer, and he saw that he had low fuel.

"Damn, love, I gotta get some gas," he whispered, and he stared at the needle, pointing to "E." He watched as she slowly bobbed her head up and down, licking the sides of his shaft just before devouring the whole thing. He peeked at the huge BP sign and decided to make a quick stop before they were left stranded on the side of the road because of an empty gas tank. As he whipped into the gas station, he tapped Ramina so she could pause their session.

"Um," she hummed as she popped his tool out of her mouth. She sat up and wiped her mouth as she looked around to make sure no one was watching. They both looked at each other and burst into laughter. "Nigga, hurry up," she said playfully.

"Yes, ma'am," he answered as he made himself decent before exiting the car. He had on his dress slacks and an open shirt, displaying his tattooed belly and designer belt. His Valentino loafers clicked the pavement with each step. As he approached the store to pay for his gas, he saw a few youngsters standing by the door. He didn't know them, but obviously, they knew who he was because before he could reach the door, one of them opened it for him.

"Respect . . ." Saint greeted as he nodded to the youngsters, making sure he made eye contact with both of them before stepping through the threshold.

When Saint made it into the store, the young man that held the door open looked over at his partner with concerned eyes. He knew who Saint was and his prominent position in the streets. Saint was the plug, and every young hustler wanted to get put into position by him. Not a lot of people knew who Saint was, but if you knew . . . you knew. Saint could change a life with the snap of his fingers, so when the young dealers saw him, he was like a real-life walking lottery ticket. They just hoped that they were lucky enough to get on his radar . . . lucky enough to be a part of Saint's team. In the streets, he was a god.

However, the thought of what was going on in the alley just a few feet away was causing concern for them. They prayed to the heavens that Saint didn't notice what they knew. One of their partners was having his way with Tay in the dirty alley. It was well known that Tay was Saint's loved one, and no one wanted to be on the opposite of Saint's wrath over her—nobody.

***

"Move your hands," the young man said harshly as he looked down at Tay. Tay was on her knees in the wet alley.

Tears were in her eyes as she took the young boy into her mouth. She felt ashamed and embarrassed, knowing she was pleasing a 16-year-old boy just to get her next fix. The young hustler had his eyes on Tay for years and never thought that he would have her in the position that she was in now. The pimply-faced teen was as black as tar, and his demented, gap-toothed smile was on display. His skinny jeans were wrapped around his ankles, and he trapped the bottom of his shirt between his chin and chest to get a clear view. His big belly hung freely as he watched his manhood disappear and reappear from the blow job. His lustful eyes were fixated on the Cuban beauty that sucked him off. Her wavy hair was something he yearned after, and it made the experience even that more exhilarating to him. He couldn't believe he had Tay blowing him. She, at one time, was the catch of the neighborhood. Her association with Saint and Zoo made her a hood trophy, a notch under his belt.

He was having the time of his life, but Tay felt disgusting. As she slurped on the fat, young thug, a wave of shame overcame her. But then the pain in her stomach reminded her of why she was doing what she was doing. She felt the cold concrete and wetness on her knees and wanted it just to be over and done with. Another sharp pain hit her once again, but this time it was much more painful. It was so painful that she grimaced, causing her to scrape her teeth across the young thug's shaft. She jerked back and shrieked in discomfort.

"Bitch, watch your teeth," he said through his clenched teeth. He frowned and stepped back, snatching his tool from Tay's mouth. She dropped her head down in humiliation as she wiped the excessive saliva from around her mouth.

"Sorry," she whispered as she tried to grab his penis once again. He aggressively slapped her hand away. He then grabbed her forcefully by her face and made her look at him.

"Don't be sorry . . . be careful," he said with a demented look in his eyes.

Tay nodded her head in understanding and then gingerly took him into her mouth again. She worked her mouth on him, hoping that he would climax soon so she could get her fix from him. He threw his head back in pleasure as he gripped the back of her head and rammed himself into her mouth. She gagged and almost threw up because he was hitting her tonsils. He held her head and went as deep as he could, blocking her airwaves as he felt himself about to explode inside of her mouth. She placed her hands on his thighs and tried to push away so she could get air, but that's when he just held her tighter while releasing himself.

"Aaaagh," he moaned as a walnut-sized glob shot into the back of her throat. He finally released his grip on her head and stepped back, shaking his tool off as the semen flung from his penis.

Tay gagged and heaved as she tried her best to catch her breath. She fell to the ground, feeling dizzy from the lack of oxygen. Tay held her chest and panted heavily as she was now on all fours like a dog, searching for air. The young hustler put his tool inside of his jeans and laughed as he saw Tay suffer just beneath him. The sight of her gagging only fed into his ego. He wasn't a good-looking guy by any means. In his mind, it was payback for all the pretty girls that dissed him throughout his life. Somehow, treating her like shit made him feel better about the rejection.

He reached into his pocket and pulled out a small pack of heroin. He tossed it on the ground. It landed just to the right of Tay. She hurried and scooped it up, yearning to feel its power rush through her veins.

The hustler walked away so that he could boast to his friends about dogging the beauty. But before he could clear the alley, he heard her voice.

"Hey! Hey! What the fuck is this, man?" Tay yelled as she stood to her feet, examining the bag.

"It's what the fuck I gave you," the young man said as he paused and looked back at her.

"Yo, what's up with you? We had a deal. This isn't a forty pack," Tay yelled in disappointment as she rushed over to him and grabbed him by his jacket. He quickly snatched away and spat in her face. He had given her a small pack that he used to provide samples to the fiends. It wasn't enough to satisfy the intense hunger of a seasoned junkie. He had planned to short her from the jump, assuming she would just be happy with what he had given her.

"What the fuck?" she yelled again, as she wiped the spit from her forehead. The hustler walked away, leaving her there dumbfounded. He returned to post up right in front of the store, where his friends were waiting.

As the young man posted up, he saw the look on his friends' faces and immediately knew something was wrong.

"Fuck wrong wit' y'all?" he asked, looking back and forth between the two guys.

But before they could answer, Saint came out of the store. As he walked out, Tay was coming from around the corner in a rage. She was about to curse the hustler out but seeing Saint made her freeze up and become speechless. She stopped dead in her tracks and looked at the only man she ever truly loved. Saint was speechless as well. He froze when he saw his "baby." Although he didn't have the same type of attraction to her that she had for him, he did truly love her. He had more of a big brother feeling for her, and seeing her in her current state broke his heart into tiny little pieces. He looked at her eyes and knew that she had been using. The way they were sunk in and the dark circles were a dead giveaway that she was on the hunt for a fix.

Saint opened his mouth to speak, but nothing came out. He was watching his little baby tweaking, and it killed him. Tay could feel the awkwardness and just wanted to run away in pure disgrace. However, the pains in her stomach made her brush past him and approach the guy that had shorted her. Saint watched as she flew past him, and his eyes followed her as she stood in front of the group of guys. Saint took a deep breath and headed to his car and pumped the gas.

Damn, she looks so bad. Li'l baby don't even look like herself, he thought to himself, referring to her as a name he used to call her. He gave her that name because she was so tiny. Although she was 20, she had the body of a little boy. She had very small breasts and wasn't curvy at all. However, her pure beauty overcompensated for her lack of voluptuousness. Tay was his little baby, and that title had so many layers that only they understood.

He shook his head as if he were trying to shake off the concern that he had for her. But it didn't work. That love was embedded deep in his heart, and no matter how he tried to dismiss it, he couldn't. He glanced back and tried to see what was going on. He saw that they were arguing, but he knew that he couldn't get into another person's street business. He could tell in her eyes that she was fighting inner demons, and this crushed him to the core.

As he pumped the gas, he kept wanting to go and just save her, but he knew it was too late. His name was too good in the streets to break the code of it. He couldn't see himself trying to save a mere dope fiend from some petty business that wasn't his own. No matter how he cut it, it would seem as if he were being a square if he intervened.

He hopped back into the car. Ramina was sipping on the bottle of champagne and jamming to the music that she had turned up. The sounds of his speakers knocked as smooth R&B music sounded. The chill ambiance of Summer Walker's song had her in her element. She swayed back and forth with her eyes closed while snapping her fingers to the beat. She was oblivious to what was going on outside of the car and was in her own world. Saint hopped in with a heavy heart. He wanted to tell Ramina about what he saw, but he knew that it was a tender topic, so he decided to keep it to himself. He gave her a half smile and put the car in drive just before pulling off. Ramina finished off the bottle and looked over to Saint with bedroom eyes. She now wanted to finish what she had started as she looked down at his pelvic area.

"Let me get you together, babe," she said as she tossed the empty bottle in the back and then leaned forward. She licked her lips as she unbuckled his pants once again. She pulled his slightly erect tool out and circled his tip with her tongue. She knew from experience that had always got him to stand straight up in no time.

Saint drove and tried to focus on what Ramina was doing to him, but his mind was on Tay. He glanced in the rearview mirror, trying to see her, but they had gotten too far down the road. He thought that she was out of his system, but the connection was obviously still there. The look in her eyes . . . He couldn't shake those eyes. Those pretty eyes and the hurt behind them tugged at his heart. *Where did I go wrong with li'l baby? It wasn't supposed to be like this,* he thought as the guilt mixed in with heartbreak and played with his emotions. His mind drifted, and he replayed all the scenarios where he could have done something differently. As Ramina continued to work on him below, the heaviness of his heart pushed water out of his eyes. He couldn't understand why the girl's soul was tied to his like it was. No matter how hard he wanted to let her go, he just couldn't. He felt responsible for Tay's happiness, and anything beneath that felt like a failure on his part.

Ramina abruptly stopped and sat up. She looked over at Saint to see what was wrong with him. He had gone soft, and that was never a problem for him. He stood tall every single time, and his dick would get hard if she so much as touched it. But she knew what was wrong. It was written all over her man's face, and the water in his eyes was a clear indication of what she already knew. She crossed her arms as she looked straightforward, her mind churning as conflict manifested in her soul.

"Go get her," Ramina said reluctantly. She had seen Tay when they pulled up and saw their interaction as well. She decided to pretend that she didn't see it, not wanting to ruin her wedding day. But it was evident that something was bothering Saint. Ramina loved him so much that she was willing to hurt so he could be happy. Saving Tay would make him happy, and Ramina had accepted that. She knew the love that he had for Tay and seeing his pain really did something to her.

"What?" Saint said as he put his tool back in his pants. He looked at her, confused. It was as if she were reading his mind.

"You heard me. Go get your li'l baby," she said as she looked over at him, leaned forward, and gently cupped his face. "I understand. Go back," she whispered.

"I'm so sorry, love," Saint said, as he looked into his wife's eyes. A single tear slid down his face, and it simply broke Ramina's heart. She felt water build up in her eyes as the sorrow in her chest created a feeling of anxiety.

"It's fine. Turn around," she whispered, as she sat back in her seat and looked away just as the tear fell . . . just in time so that Saint didn't notice. He quickly hit a U-turn and headed back to the gas station to rescue Tay.

"You betta get outta my mu'fuckin' face. Take that pack and handle your business. You lucky I gave you what I gave you for that whack-ass head you gave me," the fat thug said as he looked at Tay with disgust. She had been begging him for the past five minutes, and he was growing agitated by her audacity.

"That's not fair. Now, give me what you owe," Tay said with pure rage as she balled up her fists and tears fell from her eyes. She knew that she would be in for a night of pain if she didn't get enough to keep the monkey off her back. What he had given her wasn't going to cut it. She needed more dope. She needed it bad and would do anything to get it.

"I'll do whatever you want me to do. Just please give me enough to shake this pain," Tay begged as an intense pain shot through her stomach once again.

The fat thug seemed as if Tay's agony amused him. He was about to push her away, but he got an idea when he saw the desperation in her eyes.

"Let my boys hit it. If you let all of us hit that pussy, you can have this," he said as he dug into his pocket and pulled out a pack. Instantly, Tay cried harder, knowing that she couldn't oblige to his request.

"I'm sorry, I can't do that," she said as she dropped to her knees in shame and teared up.

"This nasty bitch on her period," the fat thug said as he looked at his boys and laughed.

"That mouth still work, though," one of the other boys suggested.

"You damn right. That mouth works just fine," the fat thug said as he smirked and grabbed his junk and rubbed it through his jeans, thinking about the round two of action he was about to get.

"Okay, I will suck off all three of y'all. Just give me the dope first, so I know you're serious," Tay pleaded as she looked up with her hands clasped in a praying position. The fat thug reached into his pocket and pulled out a forty pack. He then tossed it on the ground where Tay was kneeling. She hurriedly scooped up the pack and it put it in her pocket.

"Come on," she said as she wiped away her tears and headed toward the alley.

The boys childishly chuckled and followed her into the darkness.

"I'm first, my nigga," one of the boys yelled as he pulled out his semi-erect penis and walked over to Tay, who was already on her knees. They didn't even notice the Range Rover pull up a few yards away. Saint smoothly stepped out and approached the alley. The sound of his calm, deep voice sounded.

"Show is over," Saint calmly said as he brushed past the two waiting thugs and headed over to Tay and the guy that she was about blow. He grabbed Tay by the arm and forcefully lifted her to her feet.

"Saint, let me go!" Tay yelled as she thought about getting her fix over anything else. Saint gave Tay a stern look as he gripped her tighter and pulled her close. She quickly backed down, knowing that Saint wasn't someone to play with. He had the savage look of a lion in his eyes, and it instantly sent chills down Tay's spine. After a few seconds of silence, Saint guided her past the crew and toward his car.

"Nigga trying to save the bitch. She belongs to the streets, my nigga," the fat thug said playfully while Saint's back was turned. The two other boys were shocked that he said something sideways to Saint. Their eyes grew as big as golf balls by their comrade's remark. One of the boys even tapped the fat thug and whispered, "What the fuck, man?" They understood who Saint was, but obviously, their friend didn't.

Saint heard what was said as he put Tay in the backseat. He remained quiet until he got her inside secure and shut the door. Then he calmly turned around and slid his hands in his pockets. He slowly walked over to the group of boys with a slight smile.

"What's your name?" Saint asked as he approached the fat one.

"I'm Fatboy," the guy proudly said as he poked his chest out a tad bit more than it already was.

"You know who I am?" Saint asked as he stepped closer to Fatboy, chest to chest.

"Nah, not really. *Should* I know?" Fatboy asked sarcastically.

"I know," one of the other boys said as he nervously raised his hand. They knew Fatboy wasn't aware of who Saint was. He had been locked up for the past few summers. Saint quickly put his finger to his lips, signaling that the boy should be quiet.

"My name is Saint. I didn't mean any disrespect, li'l nigga. This business is personal and—"

"Li'l nigga?" Fatboy said, cutting Saint off. He looked around at his boys like he couldn't believe what was said to him. He slid his hand into his back pocket and grabbed the small .25-caliber pistol out and transferred it into his front pocket. He intentionally wanted Saint to see what he had. He then continued. "I'm big weight out here. I advise you to take yo' ass where you came from. What you, a deacon or something?" he asked as he looked Saint up and down and saw his attire, not knowing that it was his wedding day.

"Nah, beloved. I'm no deacon. But check this out . . . You got it. You won. I apologize for the misunderstanding," Saint said politely, as he slowly put his hand on Fatboy's shoulder and patted it one time. "Have a good night, gentlemen," Saint said without one bit of malice or aggressiveness in his tone. He simply just patted the boy's shoulder and turned to walk away. He looked over to his left and saw Zoo creeping from their blind side. He didn't even bother to look over directly at Zoo. It was business as usual for them. Minutes before, Saint had called him and told him what was going down with Tay. Zoo had been parked on the side, watching the whole thing play out.

As Saint got to his car door, Zoo was preparing to blow Fatboy's brains out. Zoo knew exactly who to hit because of the discreet signal that Saint had given him by merely tapping the shoulder of Fatboy. He was nonverbally giving Zoo the greenlight. As Saint drove off, a loud thud rang off in the distance. It was the sound of a single gunshot that resonated, echoing through the air. Saint and Ramina didn't flinch at the noise, already knowing the cause of it. Tay jumped, frightened, and tried to see what was going on, but Saint had already pulled out of the lot and out of eyeshot of the homicide. In the streets, Saint was feared, and his reputation was something that he would guard with his life. Too bad Fatboy didn't know any better. He would now have to find out about who Saint was on the *other* side . . . because he was clueless in this realm.

Chapter Three

Toad You

Ramina cried a cascade of tears as she sped down the highway, pushing nearly eighty miles per hour. The top was dropped as she glided in and out of lanes on the interstate. She needed to feel the force of the wind. She wanted to *feel* it. She had to feel something . . . something other than what she was feeling on that early morning. Everything was just so heavy on her soul, heavier than anything had ever been. Her entire being was shaken, and everything that she knew was for certain somehow was now unreliable. The picture-perfect life that she finally thought she had seemed to be snatched from under her. The only man that she truly loved was in love with someone else. She could tell. She just knew. There was something about seeing those tears in Saint's eyes that told her the truth. Not his words or his actions, but those tears told her everything that she *didn't* want to know. She had been with him for years and never once saw tears from that man.

Ramina had no makeup on her face, and her natural brown skin glowed in the sunlight. Being in public like this was a rarity for her. She hadn't walked out of the house in years without being dolled up. But on this day, she just had to get away from the anguish that was back home.

She slightly raised her oversized sunglasses with her index finger and wiped tears away as she wept. She cried uncontrollably as she thought about how her husband was at home tending to that dope-sick woman, rather than celebrating their new marriage with her. The loud purr from her silver Porsche Panamera ripped through the airwaves. She neared one hundred miles per hour. The sounds of Lauryn Hill knocked through her sound system as her long, jet-black hair blew wildly in the air.

She was supposed to be on an airplane on her way to Italy for her honeymoon. Instead, she was in still in the bayou . . . heartbroken. She was there wondering if she had made a mistake by marrying Saint. *How can he be trying to put her together, while I'm fucking falling apart?* she thought as the tears continued to flow. She had loved Saint with every morsel in her body, and she knew he was a good man. The problem was that he was being a good man to someone else. Anxiety crept in. Although she tried to breathe slowly, the heartache was overweighing it all.

"Why does he love her? I fucking hate her. I *hate* that bitch. I wish she would just die," Ramina cried as she smashed the accelerator to the floor, pushing the luxury vehicle to the limit. She was now nearing one hundred twenty miles per hour. Somehow, the speed seemed to help her release the unwanted tension that had built up inside of her.

Ramina's disappointment and frustration had reached its boiling point. She felt like she was being robbed—robbed of the life that she had deserved. She stood by Saint's side and played her position the right way throughout the years. The pain slowly started to become rage. She possessed a massive flame that burned deep within her soul, all behind the man that the streets feared, and the ladies lusted after. She was drawn to his quiet power. She was addicted to him, and she wasn't going to let him go.

"Fuck that!" she yelled as she squeezed the steering wheel as tightly as her grips would allow. She let out a roar of passion that she never knew she had.

"Aaaagh!" she screamed, which turned into a gut-wrenching sob. She angrily hit her steering wheel. She wasn't a hateful person, but over that man, she would become the worst. He was her trigger. *He was her trigger.*

She felt something in the pit of her stomach rumble as nausea set in. Suddenly, the urge to throw up overwhelmed her. She was sweating profusely and dry heaving while becoming dizzy. Vomit came up in her mouth. She leaned over to spit the vomit out in her passenger seat. Her eyes grew as big as golf balls when she saw all the clear secretions that she had thrown up. But it wasn't the spit and secretions that alerted her. It was the small green frog hopping around in it, struggling to escape the thick liquid . . .

What the fuck? she thought as she tried to refocus her fuzzy vision. Her heart raced rapidly. She was confused and frightened at the same time. She shook her head and focused on the road . . . but it was too late.

The sound of a thunderous crash resonated in the air, followed by screeching tires and crushing metal. Ramina crashed her car into the back of an eighteen-wheeler semitruck, instantly propelling her body into the air like a rag doll. She was launched about fifty yards and crashed violently onto the pavement. Her body rolled over a dozen times against the concrete, ripping her flesh with each flip. It all happened so fast . . . She never saw it coming. She didn't have a chance. As Ramina lay there slipping in and out of consciousness, she was completely bloodied, and the left side of her face was skinned from skidding on the road. She tried to move, but she couldn't. The broken bones and trauma wouldn't allow her to.

She felt her life slip away, and all she could think about was Saint. She just wanted him to come and save her. She wanted him to make sure that she would make it through. Her thoughts went to Tay. Her eyes were getting heavy as her vision got blurry, and she saw an animal standing over her. She was horrified, yet she could not gasp, scream, or move. She was just there. It looked like a monkey, but she wasn't sure. She couldn't really make it out clearly. She thought that it was odd. She had never seen that type of animal up close other than in zoos, and that was behind glass. Ramina took a deep breath as her eyes slowly closed. She couldn't fight the urge to sleep . . . So she let go.

Saint sat in the chair next to the bedside of Tay. He watched closely as Tay scratched her body vigorously and fidgeted in her sleep. Her body was drenched in sweat as if a bucket of water had been dumped on her. She faintly whimpered, and she continually clawed at herself. She scratched so hard that she drew blood, making thick welts on her arms and neck, and trickles of blood were in different spots on the white sheets. Saint understood what was happening to Tay and knew there was nothing he could do about it, but just wait it out. Her body was going through withdrawals, and it yearned for the drug that made Saint wealthy. Saint was sitting in a chair right next to the bed and watched, knowing that he was helpless, and that's what broke his heart. He wasn't that much older than Tay, but in a way, he felt like she was his little baby. He felt the responsibility of taking care of her, no matter how difficult it was.

Something deep inside was telling him that he was doing the right thing. He rubbed her hair, gently laying it down and brushing it in one direction. He could feel the wetness from the sweat, but he didn't care. He just wanted her to get better. He slowly caressed her and whispered to her. "Shhh . . . shhh," he said, trying to comfort her, and instantly he noticed the murmurs slowed, and her body got more relaxed. "That's my girl," he whispered as he leaned over and tenderly kissed her forehead. He continued to rub her until she stopped tweaking altogether. He half-grinned while watching her closely. He knew that she was a diamond in the rough and had the potential to be something great. However, her past demons had a hold on her, a strong one. She had been through so much in her life, and he knew that if he didn't help her, no one else would. At 21, she had suffered three lifetime's worth of pain and despair. Her pure beauty hid her pain well, and she looked nothing like what she had been through.

His thoughts drifted to his new wife, and guilt set in. The thought of him asking her to go through this at the time of their wedding really bothered him. He felt selfish, knowing that he temporarily ignored her feelings to tend to Tay, who had a hold on him, and he could not understand why. He thought that he was the cause of her current struggle, so, therefore, he felt responsible for her. He hadn't seen her in over a year, but there wasn't a day that passed that he didn't think of her. When he saw her in that alley, he felt God was giving him a second chance to right his wrongs with her.

Although he had her blessings to help Tay, he knew deep inside that Mi had put his feelings before her own. He was so worried about Tay that he never thought about how Mi must've felt. He understood that she hadn't deserved to be anyone's second option or on a back burner.

He felt a flutter in his heart as if he just saw Ramina's face. He shook his head, ashamed of himself, and headed out of the room to tell her he was sorry. He hadn't even realized he had been in the guest room with Tay all night. Not until he saw the rays of the sunlight peeking from the living room blinds did he notice that he had broken day while tending to her.

He walked across his spacious home, and it felt unusually cold. The ten thousand-square foot estate was one that Mi had made their home. Her woman's touch shined through the exquisite interior design. Her stellar creativity was one of the many things he loved about her. It was simply beautiful. Saint walked across the marble floors and looked up at the high ceiling. Beautiful baby saints were hand drawn on his ceilings. He was amazed every time he looked at it. It was Ramina's idea, and it added character to the home. It was like their mini Vatican with beautiful brown faces rather than pale ones. He reached the porcelain wraparound stairs that led to the second floor and headed toward their bedroom.

When he walked in, he expected to see Ramina in the mirror, doing her hair and makeup as she did every morning. He entered, ready to apologize for his actions, but he found himself standing there alone. The bed was perfectly made up, and the room was empty. A small note was on the bed with her handwriting on it. Just next to the note were two first-class tickets to Italy. As he read through the paper, tears formed in his eyes, but none fell. Her words seemed to talk directly to his heart. He dropped his head and thought back to how it all began. He thought about how times had changed over the past few years. He sat on the bed and just stared at the paper in disbelief. At the time, he thought that it was the beginning of a new chapter in his life. Now, looking back, he realized it was a part of the ending. He wished he had never been opened to the things that Cuba offered.

He sat on the bed and thought deeply. He remembered when things were so simple, and life seemed easy. He looked to his left and saw a Bible there. It had a sticky note with Ramina's handwriting on it. It simply read,

Give this to her . . . Matthew 11:28–30

He grabbed the Bible, stood up, and walked back to the room where Tay was. She was still in there fighting her demons and sweating profusely as she slept in obvious agony. There was an onslaught of moaning and scratching as she clawed and dug into her own skin. It was hard for Saint to watch, but he knew that she had to go through the withdrawal process to get better eventually.

He wanted to run out and find Ramina, though he knew that Tay really needed him. He was torn. Deep down in his soul, he recognized that the right thing to do was to go after his newly wedded wife. But what about Tay? What was she supposed to do without any help? She had no one in the entire world except him.

Saint looked at his li'l baby in pain, and it shook him to his core. At that moment, he realized that he truly loved her. It was because of the way she made him feel and the emotion that she pulled out of him. It wasn't a romantic relationship at all . . . Well, not in Saint's eyes. It was a complicated love between those two. Deep in his heart, he felt that he was responsible for her happiness. That was a heavy burden for anyone to have, but he knew that he owned it. He could not wrap his mind around his bond with her. It felt as if he were rooted to this girl. From the surface, it appeared as if it were a brother/sister relationship, but from Saint's point of view, he wanted to protect her as if she were his daughter. But the truth was, Tay looked at him as more than that. She was deeply in love with him, and he realized that. That's why the relationship was so toxic. His mind drifted back to the first time he met her in Cuba. It was the night that his life changed forever.

Chapter Four

Lion and Water

Two Years Before . . .

The sun was just rising, and the orange and purple hues blended perfectly on the sky's horizon. Blue water from the waves washed up on the shore and wet the entire backside of Ramina. She lay on the edge of the beach shore, just close enough to feel the water wash up. She wore a sheer cover-up robe that left nothing for the imagination. Her wide hips were on full display as she parted her thick brown thighs. Saint lay naked, right in between her legs, kissing her gently. Her red, pedicured toes were dangling in the air as she gripped the sand while gasping for air.

Ramina arched her back and moaned as Saint slowly rocked in and out of her cleanly shaven love box. He took his time, as usual, rocking back and forth, making sure he stayed deep inside of her while doing so. Ramina couldn't help to be in love. The man that was making love to her was her soul mate. Everything about Saint was perfect for her liking. His size, his girth, and his rhythm were tailor-made. It seemed as if he had been specially made for her. She loved the way he made love to her. He was never loud, he never went fast, and he was never weak. She could feel his power in each and every stroke . . . every time. She loved the weight that he put on her when they were intimate. For some odd reason, it comforted her and made her feel safe. As Saint rocked back and forth, he placed his lips by her left earlobe and whispered everything he wanted her to know. Saint was skilled and seasoned enough to know that anything you wanted to stick in a woman's thoughts had to be said during sex . . . good sex, that is. It was seduction at its highest level.

"You are my soul mate," he said in his deep baritone as the sound of the ocean echoed through the air. It was a perfect combination, his voice and nature's ambiance. Earlier that morning, he had wakened her up with kisses and, shortly after, walked her to the beach. They were just outside a private villa in Aruba. It sat directly on the beach, and Saint took full advantage of the majestic layout. He wanted to celebrate her birthday correctly, so he took her international to hail her special day. Saint and Ramina had traveled the world together and made love on different beaches around the globe. It was "their thing." They traveled several times a year and lived life to the fullest. They had been together since they were teens, and they deserved it . . . They deserved each other. Their passports were stamped up and barely had room for any more.

He gently lifted off her so that he was looking her directly into her eyes. He stretched out his arms, flexing his muscles as he repositioned himself while remaining deep inside, touching her bottom. He continued stroking her with a slow, constant pace . . . making sure he stayed at the back of her love box. He was applying that pressure, that heaviness that kept her clitoris engaged. Ramina stared at him intensely and thought about all the reasons why she was so in love with her man . . . her lion. She loved the way his full beard hung like a mane. His belly slightly poked out, but as she glanced down, she could still see him sliding in and out of her. Saint gradually changed pace, giving her longer strokes. She grabbed the back of his neck and raised her knees, pulling them back closer to her chest, thus, giving him more access to her.

She mouthed, "I love you," as a tear rolled down her face, feeling overwhelmed by his pure love and energy. Saint was just different. She had never cried while making love before she met Saint, but with him, it happened almost every time. They were not tears of pain, discomfort, or even of the slightest sorrow. She cried because she was elated. She cried because she knew that he loved her without any bias. His love was unwavering, intentional, and most of all, it was unconditional. The way he looked at her while he sexed her was almost hypnotizing. He never looked away or was embarrassed. The constant eye contact made it more dreamlike. He stared at her while slowly tapping her. This was a nonverbal language that gave her a sense of security. His confidence gave her strength, and this exchanging of energy always was food for her soul.

"Saint, I love you so much. You . . . You feel so good, baby," she moaned as the tears steadily flowed. She smiled while biting her bottom lip in pleasure. Saint's constant stroking and patience were about to pay off. He had been building up her climax for the past twenty-five minutes, and she could feel her release nearing. She adored the way he handled her. He was never rough with her; always patient.

Saint stared into his woman's eyes, and the way her breathing became rapid, he knew she was about to reach her orgasm. He ran his tongue across his lips as he felt his tool get even more erect. The sight of her curvy body and big breasts turned him on. Her dark areoles were huge, and he saw them beginning to get erect as well. He loved the way they jiggled with every thrust. He listened carefully as she whispered in between gasps.

"I'm about to come . . . I'm about to come. Don't stop. Please, don't stop," she said as she gripped his forearms and dug her nails into them.

Saint wasn't a rookie by any means, so he stayed the course and didn't change up his rhythm. Through experience, he knew that when a woman tells you she is about to have an orgasm, the last thing you do is speed up. That was a novice mistake that most men made. They had no patience. Saint had plenty. He didn't do anything fast. He understood that you should keep the same speed and stay at the same spot when a woman is reaching her boiling point. So that's exactly what he did. He steadily glided in and out of her until he felt her vagina walls contract and get tight around his pole. Ramina's body jerked violently, and that's when he knew she was there. He slid his pole out of her and tapped her clitoris swiftly with his tip. After a few hard taps, a geyser of liquid shot from her box and crashed against Saint's stomach.

"Aaaagh," she yelled loudly as she let herself go, squirting everywhere. The wet sensation made Saint explode as well. He shot his load on her belly as her final squirts seeped out. They had climaxed together and found themselves on their backs, looking at the sun come out. It was a beautiful thing. It was perfect timing.

"Happy birthday, pretty girl," Saint said as he held out his hand. Ramina breathed hard and tried to catch her breath before speaking. She couldn't help but smile.

"Thanks, baby," she answered as she slapped hands with her man. They had an unbreakable bond. Although they were lovers, they were best friends.

"I'm hungry," Ramina said as she looked over at him.

"Bitch, me too," Saint playfully said as he displayed his beautiful smile. Then both of them burst out into laughter, and Ramina rolled over and straddled him, playfully hitting him. She leaned down and kissed him after they play fought.

"This really was beautiful. It means the world to me," she said, thinking about their vacation and the thought he put into it. She was on cloud nine.

"And you mean the world to me, pretty girl," Saint answered.

Saint watched as Ramina did her makeup in the mirror across the room. She sat in front of a vanity mirror as she swayed to the music playing in the background. She wore a huge terry cloth robe with a towel wrapped around her head. The smell of sage filled the room, and the smoke danced in the air freely, setting the vibe. Saint sat at the dining table in the middle of the villa. His focus was on the scattered dead men's faces that were on the table. He put the stack of hundred-dollar bills through the money machine and watched as the Benjamin Franklin faces flickered one after another. A loud beep sounded, letting him know that the count was complete. He quickly grabbed the money out of the top of the machine and then wrapped a rubber band around it. He neatly placed the stack in the duffle bag that was near his feet. He always recounted the money to make sure it was right. He wanted to make sure that his purchase money was accurate for his upcoming Cuba trip. Although they were in Aruba that morning, he planned on being in Cuba by the end of the night. Saint had been in the drug game since his teens, but everything changed when he found a heroin connect in Havana, Cuba, while on vacation with Ramina. He had the plug going on seven years, and his empire had skyrocketed since the pipeline was formed. He always scheduled his Cuba trips at the end of a vacation that he and Ramina took. That way, he could avoid the hassle of the US and being under the watchful eyes of the American government. Saint was very strategic, and this was just one of his cautious tactics to remain meticulous.

"So, listen. I'm going to meet you back here in two days. I'm going to shoot this move and be right back," he said as he zipped up the duffle bag.

"OK, babe, I'll be here waiting," Ramina answered as she applied the blush on her cheekbones. She paused and turned around so she could be facing him rather than the mirror. She watched as he walked over to her with his duffle bag in hand. He had a stack of money in his hand and gave it to her.

"This is for some shopping. Zoo is downstairs when you're ready to go. Just call him, and he'll have the car ready for you out front," Saint said, letting her know that he had everything taken care of. Zoo always tagged along with them when they traveled the world.

The car service was waiting outside of the villa to transport him to the private airport. As usual, he chartered a private plane to Cuba so he could meet his connect Alejandro. Ramina took the money and smiled as she examined the stack. She loved the way he spoiled her, and she couldn't wait to hit the shopping district in downtown Aruba. She stood up and jumped into his arms, instantly making him drop his bag. She wrapped her legs around his waist and wrapped her arms around the back of his neck. Saint was just under six feet, so he hovered over her five foot four frame. It was easy for him to scoop her up as he cuffed her plump butt cheeks, feeling her wobbly, soft cheeks.

"My pretty girl," he whispered as he hugged her tightly. She closed her eyes and inhaled the clean, fresh smell of his cologne.

"You're so good to me. Thank you, baby," she said just before she leaned in and kissed him. After their kiss, he let her down to her feet and just stared at her, smiling. She always loved it when he showed his teeth. It was her favorite part of his physical features. The sight alone made her want to have a replay of what they had done earlier that morning.

"You deserve to be treated well. You're perfect. Perfect for me, anyway. You just get a nigga, ya heard me?" Saint said with sincerity.

"You heard me?" Ramina mocked while smiling from ear to ear and playfully making a silly face. She loved mocking his New Orleans accent. His charm melted her, and he didn't even try. It was so effortless with Saint. He always knew how to time things perfectly to make her smile. That Creole-influenced twang got her every time. They both laughed.

"Be safe. I'll be here waiting when you get back," she said as she stood on her tiptoes to give him a peck on the lips. Saint gently smacked her buttocks and squeezed it just before he picked up the duffle bag, heading out the door.

"Forty-eight hours," Saint said as he opened the door to exit.

"Forty-eight hours," Ramina repeated as she stared into the mirror, beginning to apply her mascara. That was something they always said before he went on his Cuba trips. He always made it a brief trip when going to visit his plug.

"Hey," Saint said as he looked back at his woman.

"Yes," she said as she stayed focused on the mirror while tending to her eyelashes.

"Look at me," Saint instructed. He waited until her full focus was on him before he spoke again. Ramina slowly turned toward him and caught him staring at her, smiling widely. His whites and his golds instantly made her smile.

"Yes?" she said beaming.

"I just wanted to look at you again," he said as he stared at her in admiration. After a few seconds of gazing, he quickly left. She sat there, blushing with butterflies in her stomach, staring at the door.

"That's a man right there," she whispered to herself as she shook her head in disbelief at how he could still make her feel like a little girl. His charisma always made Ramina feel a type of way and only solidified that he was the love of her life.

Saint took the elevator to the lobby and checked his watch to see what time it was. Just like he planned, he was in the lobby at nine a.m. sharp. The private resort had some of the best villas in the country, and it was one of Saint's frequent vacationing spots. He walked onto the marble floors that led to the spacious, open lobby where staff moved about the place. The five-star establishment was gorgeous, and the sound of the live Mariachi band serenaded the morning guests. Saint wore an open linen shirt with Armani slacks, Italian cut. As he walked out on the marble floor, he looked over toward the car and saw Zoo sitting there conversing with a beautiful Latina woman. Zoo glanced over and noticed Saint and cut his conversation short to join him.

"Top of the top," Saint smoothly said as he slid a toothpick in his mouth.

"Top of the morning," Zoo responded as he slapped hands with his best friend. They both headed outside of the establishment so they could talk away from the earshot of the other guests and staff.

"How was your night?" Saint said as he gave Zoo a smirk and looked back at the lady who was sitting at the bar.

"Nigga, you see that over there?" Zoo said as he smiled and rubbed his hands together while glancing back as well.

"I see it, for sure," Saint complimented and approved. He shook his head and chuckled at his right-hand man. They had spent the previous day on a yacht together, including the Latina woman, so he was familiar with her. She looked back and saw Saint and Zoo looking at her. She smiled and waved at Saint. Saint slightly smiled and gave her a head nod acknowledging her.

"What?" Zoo asked, knowing Saint wanted to say something. "What? Spill the beans, brody," Zoo said.

"I'm just saying . . . every trip we take, you come with a different girl. Every single time," Saint said.

"Everybody can't be like you and Ramina. See, y'all got something real. All this shit is fake, bro," Zoo explained.

"What you mean exactly?" Saint asked, trying to follow Zoo's thoughts.

"I mean that none of this is real if you really think about it. She wants me because I got the bag and can take her on trips for her to post on social media. And to be honest, I only want her because of that phat ass. Simple math. It's an unspoken transaction that no one likes to talk about," Zoo expertly explained.

"I get it, bruh. I just can't lie down with a bitch I don't have a mental connection with, ya hear me? I mean, I could when I was younger, but now, I'm on some other shit. Catching a nut is only half the pleasure," Saint said.

"I feel that. But until I find someone like that, I'm keeping my options open," said Zoo. He tapped Saint on the chest playfully and looked around like he was about to tell him a secret. "Bro, I let that bitch spit in my mouth." They both burst out into laughter, and Saint shook his head in disbelief.

"Y'all into some freaky shit. What the fuck, man?" Saint asked while laughing.

"You damn right. She loves for me to choke her while I'm hitting it," Zoo explained.

"What?" Saint asked while squinting his eyes.

"This girl is wild as hell, brody. I thought I was about to kill her last night, but she didn't want me to stop. She said she comes harder when she's about to pass out. It's the weirdest shit."

Saint just stayed silent and shook his head as he couldn't wrap his thoughts around the choking thing. He couldn't see how a woman could let a man do that to her. He tried to envision himself choking Ramina but couldn't. In his mind, during sex, a woman should be handled gently and treated like a difficult math problem. This meant slowly taking your time to figure out the intricacies that please her. He knew that sex was about breaking a body's code, not pain. This is why he could make a woman fall in love with him, while others like Zoo couldn't. Before Saint could respond, he saw a black luxury car pull up. He knew that it was for him. He arranged for the car service to pick him up at nine oh five.

"Okay, this me," Saint said as he reached out and slapped hands with Zoo.

"Bet. I'll make sure Ramina is good," Zoo ensured his right-hand man, knowing that would be the next thing Saint would say to him.

"I appreciate you. I'll be right back," Saint confirmed as the car pulled up right in front of him. One of the bellhops went to open the door, and Saint stepped forward to slide in the backseat of the vehicle. The bellhop held his hand up, signaling for Saint to pause. He then looked past him and focused on the group of four men emerging from the elevator, all white men of a certain age. They all looked to be fiftyish. They wore different variations of tropical shirts, and all had deep tans. They were chatting among themselves and had beers in their hand as they approached the car. They also were rolling luggage with their free hands.

"Excuse me, sir," the bellhop said to Saint as he slightly brushed him to the side, clearing the path for the white men approaching. Saint instantly grew offended and frowned at the lack of respect shown for him. Zoo caught wind of Saint's discomfort and immediately went into goon mode and stepped forward.

"Don't get smacked the fuck up out here," Zoo said with his face twisted up in anger.

As always, Saint remained calm and gently tapped Zoo's back and whispered, "It's all good. Stand down." He didn't want Zoo to go berserk. He knew his friend well enough to know that he had no problem with turning the small situation into a chaotic scene. Zoo took a deep breath and stepped back as Saint requested.

"Sir, I apologize, but this service is for Mr. Regis," the valet said as he didn't even take the time to look at Zoo. As the men approached, they dropped their luggage and like ants to sugar, the bellboys hustled to pick up their bags.

Who is this guy? Saint thought to himself, offended. He stepped back and closely watched as everyone seemed to want to cater to the group of men. He watched as the men all slid into the back of the spacious car, and the man with the open shirt and bone-white hair was the last to enter the vehicle. The man had a head full of white hair and a neatly trimmed goatee. His teeth were pearly white. He reached into his pocket and pulled out a diamond-encrusted money clip as he watched the last of the bags being loaded into the trunk. He then peeled off Benjamin Franklins and tipped each bellboy that was in his sight. By the way that everyone was so attentive to him, one could tell the respect level that everyone had for the man. Saint and Zoo watched as the man got inside the car and slowly cruised out of the resort's lot.

"Our money spends like his," Zoo said as he reached into his pocket and pulled out a rubber-banded knot of one-hundred-dollar bills and fifties. He waved it in their faces as he had a smug look on his face.

"Put that away," Saint said calmly and in a low tone. He then leaned over to a young valet worker and asked him the question that was on his mind.

"Who was that?" Saint questioned.

"That's Regis Epstein," he answered while leaning in and keeping his voice low. He then continued to fill in Saint. "He owns this entire resort. He actually has a few of them here and also in the United States. Big spender . . . big tipper. Everyone wants to get in his good graces to catch him on one of his generous nights. He's a fucking billionaire," the man said with excitement.

"Gotcha," Saint said while nodding, taking in the information. He then realized that it wasn't all about money. Sometimes, power.

Saint reached into his pocket and slipped the valet a hundred-dollar bill for the insight. The valet's eyes lit up, and he quickly thanked him while sliding the money into his pocket. The valet looked beyond Saint and waved over a second car to pull up. Saint followed his eyes and saw the car. He slapped hands with Zoo and watched as the valet opened the door for him.

"In a minute, beloved," Saint said to Zoo just before he smoothly slid into the backseat of the car with a duffle bag in hand. He was on his way to get on a jet to order one hundred kilos of the purest heroin in the world.